DEADLY GRIEF

RICHARD T. CAHILL JR

To Margaret Cahill -- I couldn't have done it without you, Mom.

1

It had been almost ten years since I was last in county court. In fact, I had gone out of my way to avoid it. Most of my practice focused on workers' compensation and social security disability claims, with an occasional personal injury case that wasn't gobbled up by the big firms and their silly television ads.

Granted, I had taken a few criminal cases. These were usually misdemeanors in local city court, maybe a DWI, a simple drug possession, or a traffic ticket. When you're running a small private practice, you sometimes have to take what comes. Regardless, I stayed out of county court. It brought back too many painful memories.

This day, however, I had no choice. I had been summoned by Linton County Court Judge John J. Hardy. Hardy had served for decades as the county district attorney before rising to the bench nine years earlier. He was well known for his sense of humor and jovial personality, but when Judge Hardy extended an invitation, it was unwise to be tardy or, even worse, absent.

I received the call yesterday just before closing my office for the day. Hardy's personal secretary, Ethel Bollenbacher, politely but sternly informed me that I was expected to appear before the judge at 8am sharp. No explanation was given for the summons and her tone of voice invited no inquiry. I was barely able to say, "Yes, ma'am," before she hung up the phone.

As I reached the front door of the courthouse, I wondered for the thousandth time why I was being called in. Judge Hardy had never assigned me cases before and I was not even on the felony assigned counsel list. Other attorneys I knew usually just got a phone call to advise them of the assignment. This was a personal summons and the mystery of it all had me stumped. I had worked for Judge Hardy back when he was district attorney, but I doubted he wanted to discuss old times.

"Hello, counselor," came a familiar voice as I walked through the door. It was Larry Watson, the head of court security. He was stationed in his usual chair just inside the front door with the metal detectors. Most people who entered the courthouse had to empty their pockets of all metal objects and place them in grubby plastic containers before going through the large detectors. Any remaining metal would cause a loud and shrill beep. Those causing such a sound would have to spread their arms and legs wide while the guard ran a small wand over their bodies to find the offending metal. It was a very degrading experience and I was glad that practicing attorneys with proper credentials or who knew the security staff were spared this experience.

"How ya doing, Larry?" I said as I started reaching for my attorney card.

Larry waved me off. He was retired from a career as a jail guard. Though his hair was white and his stomach slightly extended over his gun belt, Larry was still intimidating when he wanted to be. At the moment, he was smiling and came across as almost grandfatherly. "Connor, I've known you since you were just a boy. You don't need to show me your card."

I gave a quick smile. "Thanks, boss." Then it occurred to me. "Hey, Larry, you hear any talk about why Hardy wants to see me today?"

He thought for a moment. "Well, it could be the Clancy case," he offered. "The son of a bitch killed the Coleman girl."

"Oh, shit," I groaned. "That's all I fucking need."

Bob Clancy was a local lowlife who had been arrested for a variety of petty crimes over the years. Most people in the city of Rockfield knew him for his wild antics when he was drunk or high. Before he had his driver's license taken from him after his fifth or sixth drinking and driving offense, he drove his car into a delicatessen window. Since it was well after midnight and most of the city closes after eleven, the crash was heard for blocks. By the time the police arrived, Clancy was sitting on the floor eating a large Genoa salami without a care in the world.

The incident received only a small write-up in the local papers, but people talked about it all over town. As for Clancy, he suffered a few stitches in his head, and was jailed for sixty days.

As Clancy got older and his drinking and drug use worsened, he turned to burglary and petty theft to feed his habits. People stopped seeing him as a legendary wild man having fun. He was just another local bum. He ended up doing a few state bids, but always returned to Rockfield.

About a week ago, Clancy had been arrested again, but this time for murder. According to the *Rockfield Tribune*, the city's oldest newspaper, Clancy broke into a house on the outskirts of town. He strangled and stabbed the only person at home. The victim was a seventeen-year-old cheerleader named Michelle Coleman. I remembered seeing a picture of her in her cheerleading outfit on the front page. She was a pretty blonde with bright blue eyes. What a waste.

I began to think about being assigned to defend this dirtbag.

This was not the kind of publicity I needed for my practice. *Connor Phelan, Attorney at Law* had been open for only a little under a year. Business was going well, but defending a guy like Clancy was not going to bring people through the door. I was not hurting for money, but it was important to me that the practice succeed and at least pay for itself.

"Well, you better get up there, Connor. Your client awaits," Larry said with a big smile.

"Thanks a lot," I said in an overly sarcastic voice as I started walking to the elevator. It was already open, so I walked in and pressed the button for the third floor. As the door closed, I could hear Larry still snickering in appreciation of his own wit.

When the elevator finally reached the third floor, I stepped off and walked over to the judge's chambers. The door was thick wood with an opaque window. Its faded gold lettering advertised that the room belonged to the Linton County Court Judge. I opened the door and stepped into the office. It was modestly furnished with a leather couch on one side of the room for attorneys and a light brown wooden desk at the far end of the room where Miss Bollenbacher sat. She was dressed in a white blouse with a blue floral design. Her collar was fastened tightly at her neck by a large brooch made of dark stones in the shape of a butterfly. Her gray hair was styled in a very tight bun. Her appearance was very severe and matched her temperament.

"Mr. Connor," she announced. It was a statement, not a question.

"Yes, ma'am."

"Judge Hardy is waiting for you, young man," she said.

I nodded obediently, but as I walked past her to the door to the judge's inner office, I could not help feeling like a schoolmarm had just sent me to the principal's office.

I knocked and Judge Hardy's booming and boisterous voice cried out, "Come in! Come in!"

I took a breath and opened the door. Judge Hardy was seated behind his long black desk. His suit jacket and judicial robe were hanging behind him. He was wearing a crisp white shirt with a bright red tie that sort of matched his complexion. Snowy-white hair provided a real contrast with the rest of his face.

"Hello, your honor," I said respectfully.

"Ah, Connor, have a seat, my boy," he said, pointing at the two leather chairs in front of his desk. He was very polite, yet his words were clearly a command, not a request. I did as I was told.

Hardy took in a partial breath as if considering his next thought before finally saying, "Connor, I require a favor."

His choice of words was almost amusing. Hardy was one of the most powerful and influential men in all of Linton County. If he was asking for a "favor," it was really a direct order.

"Sure, judge," I replied, "What can I do for you?"

"Well, you've probably heard the terrible news about poor Michelle Coleman. Am I right?"

"Yes, sir."

"Well," the judge continued, "I have a bit of a problem. It seems that one of the attorneys assigned to this case has a conflict of interest and cannot handle it. So, I have to pick a replacement."

This beating around the bush was starting to annoy me. I decided to cut to the chase. "Your honor, if you're asking me defend this guy, I have to tell you—"

"You don't understand," the judge interrupted, "I am not asking you to defend Clancy. I want to appoint you to prosecute the murderer of Michelle Coleman."

Nothing could have prepared me for this. I had not prosecuted a case in nearly ten years. When I was in law school, I thought my entire career would be spent as a prosecutor sending violent criminals to prison for the rest of their miserable lives. Right out of law school, I took a job in the Linton County District Attorney's Office working for John Hardy himself. The job paid practically nothing, but I was on top of the world because I was a prosecutor. I did as many trials as I could. I rose quickly and, after only five years, Hardy appointed me chief assistant. Many considered me Hardy's heir apparent.

During those same five years, I met Melissa Weaver, the woman who would be my wife. She was working as an assistant district attorney prosecuting sex crimes, and was one of the most beautiful women I had ever seen. In less than six months, we were married. Two months after that, Melissa was pregnant with our son.

I had everything I ever wanted. I could not have been happier. Then, in the blink of an eye, I lost it all.

I was in court arguing a bail application when one of the bailiffs pulled me aside. Melissa had been brought to Linton Memorial Hospital. He had no details other than that it was very serious and I needed to get to the hospital right away. I drove as fast as I could and was met at the entrance of the emergency room by one of the doctors. I went completely numb as the doctor explained that my wife had a previously undetected brain aneurysm that ruptured, killing her almost instantly. She was alone when she collapsed. Melissa and my unborn son, whom we had decided to name Connor Jr., were dead before help even arrived.

As these memories flooded back to me and I started to become lost in them, Judge Hardy's voice snapped me back to reality.

"Did you hear me, Connor?"

"Yes, your honor," I croaked, trying to regain my composure.

"So, you'll do it then?" Hardy asked.

The idea of being a prosecutor again was not something I

felt ready for. I had to find a way to convince the judge without offending him. "With all due respect, your honor, isn't there someone else more qualified?" I asked.

"Nonsense, my boy," the judge said in an overly cheerful tone. "You have five years' experience as an ADA and have been a practicing attorney now for nearly sixteen years. You were my chief assistant. You could handle this murder case with your eyes closed. I'm sure once you—"

"John," I interrupted somewhat forcefully, "this is not something I really want to do. You know I haven't prosecuted a case since Melissa died."

Hardy was not used to being interrupted and certainly not to being called by his first name in chambers. Slight annoyance flashed on his face, but was quickly replaced by an attempt at an understanding smile. He paused for a moment, as if pondering his words. Then he cleared his throat and my head snapped up. I had barely realized that I had started looking at the floor.

"Connor, you know that I can just order you to do this," he said.

I started to take a breath through my mouth to respond, but Hardy held up his right hand in a clear signal for me to remain quiet.

"But I am not going to," he continued. "However, I would consider it a personal favor." He emphasized the word *personal* as if that meant all the difference.

I sat there and stared at him. It was probably only for a second or two, but it felt like ten minutes easily. Saying no to Judge Hardy was considered a mistake in Linton County. I knew if I refused, no assignments would ever come my way from his court or likely from any other court in the county. His political influence was that wide.

The idea of prosecuting a case and remembering how

everything I valued had been taken from me was not something I relished. When Melissa and my son died, I no longer had any fire left in me. I quit my job within a month and took a job with a large firm in New York City. Though I continued to be a lawyer, I focused my efforts on civil law and representing injured people. My life as a prosecutor was over.

"Connor," Hardy said, once again snapping me back to attention, "I've known you since you were knee-high to a grasshopper. I knew both your parents. I knew your wife. What happened was terrible, but it has been ten years, Connor. Ten years." He raised his voice to highlight the last two words. "Don't you think it is time to move on?" he asked. "Would Melissa want you to still mourn her death after all this time?"

I hesitated. Inside, I was becoming angry. How dare he speak her name? How the hell would this old blowhard know anything about how I felt? Had everything he cared about, his entire fucking life, his future, been taken from him without any warning? People all throughout Linton County kissed his ass on a regular basis. Hardy got everything he ever wanted handed to him on a silver platter. What did he know about pain and heartache?

As much as I wanted to tell him to go fuck himself, I quickly stifled my anger. Screaming at Judge Hardy would accomplish nothing. He could make the practice of law in this county very difficult for me. I also realized that he was right. I had been living in the past. Hell, I hadn't really been living. I'd just been going through the motions. When Melissa and I got married, we had our entire life mapped out in almost every detail. Now I was alone and living day to day without even any idea what I would order for lunch, let alone what I would do for the rest of my life.

Besides, I could just handle this one case and then go back to personal injury and workers' compensation cases. Maybe I could even get a quick plea bargain and be done with the case in a few days. It might even be good for business and bring in more clients.

I finally responded. "Okay, judge, I'll do it."

Hardy smiled and said, "You won't regret it, son."

I already did.

2

After I had reluctantly agreed to accept the assignment, Judge Hardy told me that I could pick up the prosecution's file from the district attorney's office downstairs. I decided to get it over with.

I walked through the glass doors and into the outer foyer of the DA's office. There were two secretaries sitting at metal desks. Between us was a counter with a small gate at the far end. I approached the counter and rested both my elbows on it, waiting to be recognized.

One of the two secretaries looked up at me. She was no more than twenty-five years old with light brown hair that ran far down her back. She stopped chewing gum long enough to speak with a bit of a whine. "Can I help you, sir?"

"Yes," I replied, "I'm Connor Phelan. I'm here for the Clancy file."

"Just a moment, sir," she droned, as she picked up her phone and dialed. A moment later, she spoke again. "Connor Phelan to see you, Mr. Worthington."

J. Robert Worthington III, or Rob as he was known to his friends, was the district attorney himself. He was the scion of the famous Worthington family. His grandfather, the first J. Robert Worthington, had been a congressman and his father, the only one of the three who went by his real first name, Jonas, had been county court judge until his death a few months after I left the DA's office.

It was well known that, just before he died, Jonas had gotten his son the job as chief assistant district attorney. After John Hardy was elected county judge, Rob convinced the governor to appoint him acting district attorney. Once appointed, it was no problem for sonny boy to get elected over and over again as the Worthington name was political gold. True to his name, the latest in the Worthington dynasty was an astute politician. He was well known for his press conferences prior to a trial. He would promise a vigorous prosecution and be seen both before and after a major trial. What he would almost never be seen doing was actually prosecuting a case. To the best of my knowledge, Worthington had never tried a case.

He always claimed credit for trial victories, though. When a major loss occurred, the assistant district attorney who did the trial often found himself looking for a job. As such, the attorneys who worked for Worthington almost always resolved their cases with plea bargains. Only big media cases went to trial except for those defendants who decided to roll the dice and foolishly reject sweet plea offers.

Additionally, the office was a bit of a revolving door. With no credit, plenty of blame, and almost no hope of advancement, the young assistants rarely stayed more than a year or two before seeking jobs in the private sector.

The young lady finished her call and looked back to me. "Right this way, sir. Mr. Worthington will see you now."

She pressed a button under her desk and a buzzer sounded by the gate at the end of the counter. I walked over and pushed it open. She led me down a narrow hallway barely wide enough to extend both arms. I had walked this very hallway many times. Halfway down the hall, she stopped and turned to a door on her left. Before she could knock, the door opened and District Attorney Worthington peeked out.

Worthington was tall and rather slender. He wore a navy-blue suit with subtle pinstripes and a tie that was a lighter shade of blue. His hair was thinning and was combed straight back. He had narrow round glasses that gave him the appearance of an accountant. "Hello, Mr. Phelan," he announced in a reedy voice.

I nodded and he extended his hand. As I shook it, I could not help noticing the $15,000 Rolex on his wrist. I never really understood the need to pay that kind of money for a watch. I could certainly afford it, but considered that kind of extravagance to be just plain foolish. Spending money on a classic car made sense. Spending big money on a fancy watch seemed plain silly.

Worthington signaled me to enter, so I did. His private office was much different than the rest of the district attorney's office. It had a highly waxed hardwood floor with an expensive Oriental carpet. The walls were covered with beautifully framed pictures of Worthington with numerous politicos, including the governor and even the last two presidents.

His desk was large, mahogany, and quite clearly an antique. It was truly a stunning piece of furniture. On top of the desk was a lamp and a telephone that looked like an antique, but was actually new and fully functional. The rest of the desktop was cleared and brightly polished.

Behind the desk was a leather executive-style chair with a high back. Against the wall behind the chair was a credenza of the same style and color as the desk. On that were various framed pictures that I presumed to show his wife and children.

It was obvious that Worthington liked to spend money on himself. It was also obvious that very little work was done in this office. It was a showpiece and not a real working office. The office very much reflected the man. It was also quite different than when Hardy was district attorney.

I sat down on one of the two chairs in front of the desk. Although the chairs looked as impressive as the rest of the office, the chair was decidedly uncomfortable. It was also made in a way that left the user sitting in a very low position so that Worthington would be looking down from his plush chair. It was such an obvious ploy that I almost laughed.

As he sat down, Worthington sighed. "Well, Mr. Phelan, this is really an open-and-shut case. The defendant's fingerprints were found in the house. A neighbor saw him climbing out of a window and he was caught selling some of the jewelry taken from the house. There is very little doubt that Clancy strangled and stabbed the poor girl."

"He choked her and stabbed her?" I asked.

"Yup, murder by multiple choice," he said with a little smile, obviously amused by his lousy joke.

Before he could continue, I decided to get straight to the point. "So, may I have the file?"

Worthington smiled. "Of course, Mr. Phelan." However, he did not move at all to get it, choosing instead to just keep talking. "Before we were conflicted out, we had put together a very strong case. But since Chief Assistant Alexander used to be with the public defender's office and once represented Clancy, I guess I don't get to prosecute this one."

As he said this, it occurred to me that I had neglected to ask Judge Hardy why Worthington's office could not handle the file. Now it made sense. Fred Alexander was the current chief assistant and had been with the county public defender's office for many years previously. If he had represented Clancy on prior cases, the law would not allow Worthington's office to handle the file.

I nodded, but Worthington just stared at me, as if expecting me to say something. Since I had nothing to say, the room filled with palpable silence. Finally, Worthington inhaled sharply. "Well," he said, placing both his hands on the desk, "let's get you that file."

He pressed a button on his fake antique phone and announced, "Bring in the Clancy file, please."

"Yes, sir," a powerful voice from the phone answered.

I recognized it right away as the voice of Roger Billingsley, the longtime chief investigator for the Linton County District Attorney's Office. Billingsley, or Bills as his friends called him, retired from the Rockfield Police Department after serving for twenty years. He was immediately snapped up by then DA John Hardy to be his chief investigator. He had been there ever since.

I knew from my five years in the office that Bills was a man to be respected and trusted. He had incredible instincts when it came to evaluating people. He had an innate ability to recognize a liar or a phony. I had always made sure in every one of my trials as a prosecutor to have Bills at the table with me during jury selection. He always knew the right juror to keep and the right one to send packing.

I was still thinking about one of those old trials when the office door opened and Bills walked in carrying a small folder. He was a little more gray than I remembered, but still had that dominating presence about him.

Bills held out the file to Worthington, but the district attorney waived him off dismissively and pointed at me. A big smile creased Bills's face. "Connor Phelan, how you doing, boy?" he asked jovially, extending his hand.

I stood, offered my hand, and watched it completely disappear into his catcher's mitt of a hand. "I'm okay, old man," I answered. "Aren't you ever going to retire?"

"I'm not that old, kid," Bills replied, squeezing his grip just enough to bring me up on my toes.

Before we could continue our conversation, DA Worthington's annoying voice interrupted. "Chief Investigator Billingsley," he said formally, "Mr. Phelan and I are just concluding business. Would you wait outside, please? When we are done, you can escort Mr. Phelan out."

Bills released my hand, stood up very straight, and answered, "Yes, sir," before leaving the office.

Worthington's condescending attitude toward Bills made me want to jump up and smack him. I decided not to do so. Instead, I smiled at the arrogant man and said, "Well, Mr. Worthington, now that I have the file I need, I guess I'll be on my way."

I stood up and started to leave, but Worthington quickly rose and met me at the door. "Mr. Phelan," he said insistently, "please keep me apprised on the status of the case. My office may not technically be able to prosecute Mr. Clancy, but I consider this matter still to be under my supervision."

Unable to keep smiling and resisting the urge to knock out his teeth, I looked directly at him. "Mr. Worthington, I only took this case as a favor to John Hardy. But now that I have taken it, it is under my supervision, not yours." I paused for a second to let my point sink in before continuing. "Good day, sir."

Worthington said nothing as I opened the door and left the office. Bills was waiting for me and directed me to follow him further down the hallway toward the rear exit of the office used only by employees.

When we were far enough away from Worthington's palatial office, I put my hand on Bills's shoulder. "What is that fucking guy's malfunction?" I asked.

Bills snorted a quick laugh before answering. "He's a pompous ass, but he leaves us alone when it comes to the day-to-day shit. He's just pissed off that he has to let you take a murder case. No press conference glory for his fucking ego."

I laughed and we continued walking. We passed several smaller rooms and were almost at the exit when I stopped suddenly in front of one of the corner offices. The office door was closed, but the plastic sign identified the office as belonging to the "Sex Crimes Bureau Chief." This had once been Melissa's office.

As I stood there, the memory of the first time I met her came back to me. It was my first day as an assistant district attorney. I walked into her open office to introduce myself. She was on the phone talking with some defense attorney who was pleading his client's case. Her red hair hung loosely about her shoulders and her green eyes seemed to shine.

She pointed to one of the chairs in a signal for me to sit. I did so and watched this astonishing, beautiful woman talk to the man on the phone with a voice that was melodic, yet decisive and authoritative. In those thirty seconds or so she spent on the phone, I was so mesmerized that I did not even notice when she finished her call.

When I just sat there staring for God knows how long, Melissa cleared her throat to get my attention. Startled out of my funk, I came to my feet trying to speak and extending my hand. In so doing, I knocked over a styrofoam cup on Melissa's desk, spilling coffee all over her files. It was by no means my best moment.

I was still lost in the memory when a powerful voice brought me back.

"Connor, you coming?" Bills asked.

"Yeah," I answered and resumed walking as my memory faded back into the past.

Bills said nothing, but stayed with me even after we went out the rear exit. He offered to walk me to my car.

"I walked from my office, Bills."

"That's okay, Connor," the big man continued, "I have to get some cigarettes anyway."

When we left the courthouse into the cool morning air, Bills put his gigantic hand on my shoulder. "Connor, I'm sure that Worthington told you this was an open-and-shut case, right?"

"Something like that," I answered, amused that Bills had used Worthington's exact words.

"Take a close look at this one, kid," Bills admonished seriously. "My gut is telling me that Clancy is not good for this."

"Your fearless leader tells me that Clancy's prints were found at the scene of the crime," I noted sarcastically.

Bills was not amused at all. "I know all that, kid," he said, gripping my shoulder a little tighter, "but I would bet a month's salary that he didn't kill that girl."

I hadn't worked with him in many years, but I knew from the look on the big man's face that I shouldn't argue. "All right, old man, I'll take a close look at it."

With that, Bills shook my hand and turned back to the courthouse. I guess he didn't really need those cigarettes after all.

3

_____

It took me about fifteen minutes to walk the four blocks from the County Courthouse to my office on Oak Street. I could have made better time, but my mind was spinning the entire way.

Why had I agreed to take this case? I had no desire to be a prosecutor again. That part of my life ended when my wife died. Just walking by her old office had brought back memories. I knew it was too late to back out now, though. Hardy would never allow it.

Thinking about Hardy made me angry. Why had that son of a bitch insisted on assigning me to prosecute this case? He knew better than most why I quit. He was at our wedding. He had hinted repeatedly that John was a good sturdy name for our child. He had to know how this assignment would upset me. What was he thinking?

When I arrived at my office, I tried to clear my mind. I had other cases to handle and plenty of work waiting for me. I took a deep breath and walked up the stone stairs and through the heavy wooden door.

My office was in a small brick-and-stone two-story building. In the 1940s, it had been the office of Mitchell Dewitt, a prominent and powerful state senator. Since almost every major politician at that time came to the office to speak with Senator Dewitt and get his permission before making any important decisions, the building became known as "Headquarters."

Later, after Dewitt retired, the building was sold. Numerous people owned it over the years, but nothing ever seemed to last long there. Even after seventy-five years, people still called it Headquarters.

I bought it almost a year ago when I decided to open my own law office. For a little more than eight years after Melissa's death, I commuted to New York City and worked for the law firm of Wilson, Beckett, Carter, and Anderson. Every Monday, I took the Amtrak train for almost two hours down to the city. I worked constantly throughout the week before taking the two-hour train ride back to Rockfield on Friday night. Some weekends, I stayed at the office and just kept working. I had a very small studio apartment nearby, but often slept on the couch in my office.

I cannot say I ever really enjoyed working for Wilson, Beckett. The firm's primary focus was personal injury. Billboards, newspaper ads, and cheesy television commercials brought in hundreds of cases and big attorney fees. Though the work was not that interesting to me, I was good at it.

In my first three years at the firm, I won four major trials, including one with a verdict of $15 million. The case had been seen as a sure loser, but I convinced the jury otherwise. In my seventh year at the firm, I won my last and biggest trial. Our client was dying from mesothelioma, a type of cancer caused by asbestos exposure. The two companies being sued refused to negotiate, believing the case weak. Their poor judgment resulted in a verdict for the client in the amount of $65 million.

This case had one other interesting fact. The client was the uncle of my old college roommate, who told him after he got sick to come see me specifically. Because I was the attorney credited with bringing in the case, the rules of the office provided that one third of the total fee went to me. After taxes, I pocketed slightly more than $4 million.

My results and perceived dedication to the firm brought me numerous raises and accolades. I was even offered a partnership after the big verdict, but turned it down. I had absolutely no intention of making my tenure permanent. I knew deep down that I was using the firm and all the work to hide from my reality. I also knew that I was burning myself out.

One Friday afternoon, following eight years of nothing but work and long train rides, I walked into the senior partner's office and gave my notice. The firm offered me a hefty raise to stay, but I knew I needed to return home.

After two weeks, I decided to open a small practice of my own. I really didn't need the money, but understood that sitting at home binge-watching Netflix all day was not the answer either.

So I bought Headquarters and used the first floor for my office and the second floor as an apartment. It also served as office storage space.

My secretary, Casey Franklin, met me as I walked in. If she ever heard me call her my secretary, there would be hell to pay. She preferred to be called the office manager. Since she was one hell of a secretary, I let her use whatever title she wanted. I often introduced her using various titles just to get a reaction from her.

Casey was twenty-five years old. She was attractive with a toughness about her. Her hair was dark brown and shoulder length. Peeking out of each sleeve of her red blouse were colorful tattoos on her shoulders and upper arms: flowers on the right and a dog on the left. She was not highly educated, but could match wits with the best of them. When angry, she could swear like a sailor. She was not the usual law office secretary. Frankly, she was better.

"Connor, Mrs. Martinez is waiting for you in your office," she announced. "She's been driving me absolutely batshit crazy. Yesterday, she called me twelve times. I told her that I will always call her back, but she has to be more fucking patient."

Annabelle Martinez was a client with a workers' compensation claim. She had suffered a back injury five months ago and had been unable to work since. Every day brought a new complaint about her payments or medical treatment, all of which were being fought by the insurance company. Most recently had come a notice from the workers' compensation board of a hearing. It was scheduled for tomorrow.

"All right, Casey, I'll talk to her," I said.

"What a great idea," Casey said with a sarcastic smile. "No wonder you're the boss."

I chuckled as I walked toward my office. Some might think Casey insubordinate. I just enjoyed her wit. I saw a lot of my younger self in her.

Annabelle was sitting in one of the client chairs in my office. She started to stand when I entered, but I waved it off.

"Stay seated, Annabelle," I said, and then sat down in my leather chair. It was not nearly as expensive as DA Worthington's plush chair, but it was damn comfortable. Once I had a pen and legal pad ready to take notes, I looked at my client. "What can I do for you?" I asked politely.

"Mr. Connor," Annabelle replied in a thick Mexican accent. "They want to cut my money."

She was talking about her workers' compensation benefits. The carrier had filed a motion seeking to lower her payments based on a report they obtained from an independent medical examiner.

Independent medical examiners or IMEs are doctors

selected by insurance companies and paid a great deal of money to examine people seeking workers' compensation and find nothing wrong with them. Sure, there are some IMEs who provide an honest evaluation, but they tend to be the exception.

"Annabelle," I said in my best reassuring voice, "as I have told you, the law allows the carrier to rely on their doctor's report. We have a hearing tomorrow afternoon and we will take it up with the judge."

"Mr. Connor," she protested, "the doctor never examine me. He come into the room and ask me if I can bend. I say only little bit, and he say okay, and that's it. Now he write his report saying he did this big exam and say that I am faking––"

"I understand," I interrupted. "At the hearing tomorrow, the carrier will probably look to split the difference and—"

"No," she interrupted loudly, "I cannot live on that. You have to stop them."

"Annabelle," I responded, putting up my hand to signal her to be quiet, "if we do not split the difference, then we have to litigate and take depositions from the doctors. That will take at least two months. During that time, the carrier is allowed to reduce your payments to what their doctor found."

"You mean I get no money for two months?" she asked angrily.

I paused for a few seconds to make sure she was finished before I answered. "Our options are to make a deal and your payments get cut in half or we litigate it and you get no money at all for two months," I said. "Then the judge will choose either your doctor's opinion or theirs."

"So the judge could side with them even though that doctor did nothing?" she demanded.

When I nodded my head, Annabelle screamed, "This is bullshit!" before dropping her English and ranting loudly in lightning-fast Spanish.

I almost instinctively looked out my office door to where Casey was sitting. Casey spoke Spanish fluently and I often had her translate for my Spanish-speaking clients. I did not need her for this conversation, however. Though I speak very little Spanish, I nonetheless had a pretty good idea what Annabelle Martinez was saying. After a few more minutes of listening to her rant and rave, I finally had enough. I slapped my left palm down on the desk. She stopped talking, obviously startled.

"Look," I said in a voice that invited no discussion or interruption, "you don't have to tell me that the workers' comp system sucks. I know it sucks. The carrier's doctor didn't do shit, but that changes nothing—"

"Don't they care how much I am hurting?" Annabelle interrupted again with tears beginning to flow.

"No, Annabelle, they don't give a shit," I responded. "To them, you are a file number. They will do whatever they can to stop your payments and deny your treatment. They don't care if you're in pain. They don't care if you're suffering. All they care about is not having to pay you."

Annabelle just looked at me, considering what I just said. She looked down at the floor for a moment before snapping her head back up. "Fine," she said firmly, "make the fucking deal. You tell them I am sick of the bullshit." With that, she stood up and walked out.

About two minutes later, I was just turning on my desk computer when Casey knocked on my door.

"Connor, can I ask you something?" she asked.

"Always," I answered.

"I thought you said the report in Annabelle's case from the carrier's doctor was defective because they filed it late?"

I smiled. "That's right."

"So her payments are going to stay right where they are, right?"

"Yup. Tomorrow I'll make the motion and have the report tossed. Her payments won't get cut and she'll think I'm the big hero."

Casey looked confused. "Then why didn't you just tell her that?"

"Maybe if she was a little more patient and not batshit crazy, I would have," I replied facetiously, but with an absolutely straight face.

"You really are an asshole, Connor," Casey said, starting to laugh.

"I really am," I agreed.

Casey went back out of my office. She returned a few minutes later with cups of coffee. Milk and sugar for me, and just milk for her. She sat down in the same seat Annabelle Martinez used and sipped her coffee.

"So, you gonna tell me what Judge Hardy wanted?"

I drank some of the coffee. As always, it was exactly how I liked it with just the right amount of sugar. "He assigned me the Clancy murder," I said.

"Holy shit," Casey said, sitting straight up. "You have to represent that old drunk?"

"No," I answered, "he wants me to prosecute him."

Casey said nothing. She was surprised by the news, but knew enough about my past to understand that this was not something I really wanted to talk about.

We drank our coffee in silence.

When Casey finished her coffee, she stood up and announced, "Well, I guess we need to start clearing your calendar." It was a statement and not a question. I nodded in agreement. The Clancy case was going to require a great deal of time to investigate and eventually prosecute.

We spent the rest of the workday returning calls from other clients and clearing my upcoming schedule. By 4pm, my entire calendar for the next two weeks, except for the Martinez case, was covered. I intended to handle that one personally.

I told Casey that I was closing the office an hour early. After assuring her that she would still be paid for the full day, I left, taking the Clancy file with me.

4

Before going home, I decided to stop by The Cardinal, a local tavern run by my friend Eddie Astorino. Eddie was the best man at my wedding. We met in high school at a keg party. Now, over twenty years later, he was still involved with alcohol.

When I walked in, Eddie was behind the bar cleaning some glasses. He was wearing a white apron over his blue jeans and black polo shirt. His hair was shaved and had been so ever since he developed a bald spot on the top of his head.

He looked up and broke into a wide grin. "Hey, Clubber, the usual?"

Eddie had been calling me Clubber ever since our senior year in high school. On the night of the homecoming dance, Eddie came with a beautiful redhead who turned out to be the girlfriend of a large and very jealous football player. In the resulting fight, the jock ended up on the ground with a fractured jaw.

Eddie told everyone who would listen that I broke the guy's jaw with a punch. Actually, when the angry jock pulled his right hand back for a punch, I stepped forward, grabbed his arm, and swept out his right leg, causing him to fall hard to the ground. He landed on his side and his jaw hit the concrete.

It was a basic judo move. I have studied judo since I was eleven years old and had become sick and tired of being picked on by bullies who felt they could demonstrate their superiority by beating up a smart kid who was thirty pounds lighter than they were. Nonetheless, Eddie liked the story of me throwing a massive killer punch instead. Ever after, he called me Clubber.

"Yeah," I said as I sat on a barstool, "make it a double."

A moment later, a glass of Glendalough was placed before me. I took a good draw and held the liquid in my mouth for a moment before letting the smooth Irish whiskey wash down my throat.

My moment of bliss ended when Eddie asked, "You look troubled, Clubber. What's going on?"

"What makes you think anything is going on?" I asked, taking another large sip of whiskey.

Eddie laughed slightly. "Anytime you order a double, I know something's going on."

"Well," I replied hesitantly, "Judge Hardy assigned me a case that I really didn't want."

"Well that ain't fucking news," Eddie said mockingly. "Why would anyone want to defend some scumbag?"

"No," I corrected him, "he wants me to prosecute Bob Clancy."

"Well, it's about fucking time!" Eddie yelled, slamming his fist on the bar. "You always were a prosecutor and that mutt belongs in jail."

I didn't respond and instead took another gulp. This time I finished the drink.

"Come on," Eddie insisted, "this could be the best thing to happen to you in years. You don't think Mitzy would want you sulking around after all these years, do you?"

I couldn't help but laugh. Eddie always called Melissa "Mitzy." She absolutely hated it and Eddie only did it to get a rise out of her. "You're the second person to tell me that today," I said.

"I'm sure I said it better than the first fucking guy," Eddie answered.

"The first guy was the Hon. Judge John J. Hardy," I said with a bit of mocking flourish.

"Ah, fuck him," Eddie said with a grin, as he poured me a second drink.

"Yeah, fuck him," I agreed quietly.

I said nothing for a while, and slowly sipped my Glendalough. Eddie just stood there obviously waiting for me. I knew what he was waiting for, but I made him wait a few minutes until the silence was almost too much to bear. "You want to hear about the case?" I asked.

Eddie immediately put down his bar rag and pulled over a chair. "About fucking time," he said with a lopsided smile.

I told him all about my summons to see Judge Hardy and the bombshell he dropped on me. I told him about my meeting with DA Worthington in his grandiose office. Eddie listened intently, but when I recounted how Worthington treated old Bills, he could not keep quiet.

"What a fucking douchebag," he complained. "Old Bills comes in here every Friday night. He's good people." Then he smiled again and said, "You should've decked that scumbag, Clubber."

"I only do that when I'm saving your sorry ass, pal," I joked.

"So, tell me more," Eddie demanded. "Did Clancy kill that girl or what?"

"I haven't looked at the file yet," I admitted, "so I don't know."

"Well, if he did, you make sure that old drunk pays for it," Eddie offered.

"Some people think you're an old drunk," I joked again.

Eddie got a very serious look on his face. "Look, Clubber, let's get something straight. I am not an alcoholic." Eddie paused for a moment before continuing. "Alcoholics go to meetings." Then he burst into a fit of laughter. I raised my glass in a mock salute.

We talked for a while and I had one more Glendalough, though only a single, before heading for home.

As I left, Eddie gave me his usual advice. "Don't let the fuckers get you down, Clubber."

Talking with Eddie always seemed to help no matter what the problem. His "fuck the world" attitude, though overly simplistic, had its advantages.

I drove to my home on the edge of Rockfield. Though technically a city, Rockfield was more of a glorified town or village near the foothills of the Catskill Mountains. When most people think about the State of New York and hear "city," they automatically think of Manhattan and its skyscrapers. Upstate New York is very different.

Rockfield had its office buildings, courthouses, and so forth. It also had a very rural feeling about it, especially in the residential areas. My house was a log cabin-style home at the top of a hill called Mountainview Lane. It was so titled because of the impressive view of the Catskills, though it also had a view down toward Rockfield that I particularly liked.

When I left Wilson, Beckett, I needed a new place to live. Melissa and I never took the time to buy a house. Instead, we rented one from a sweet old lady who truly undercharged us on the rent. It was a quaint little house, but I knew that continuing to live there would have been a mistake. So I bought my Mountainview estate, as I like to call it. It wasn't cheap, but in addition to the great view, it was very private and very quiet. There were only a few houses on the entire street. Since the street was three miles long, it gave the impression of isolation, though neighbors could be reached in case of emergency.

After parking my Grand Cherokee in the garage, I went in and immediately changed my clothes. I am comfortable wearing a suit, but not at home. I put on a pair of old khaki shorts and a T-shirt. I donned my favorite sandals and went into the kitchen.

I made myself some dinner. I have a number of skills, but cooking is not among them. My recipes mostly consist of leftovers and frozen dinners. On tonight's potential menu were choices of leftover pizza, three days old, or a Hungry-Man's Fried Chicken dinner. Since I was indeed a hungry man, I chose the chicken and popped it into the microwave. When it was ready, I took my gourmet meal, a cold beer, and the Clancy file, and went out into the backyard. There, I have a small patio with a fire pit and two large wooden chairs. I lit a fire and sat down in my preferred chair and began to eat, drink, and read.

The file had numerous police reports, photographs, and witness statements. They all told a consistent story. Michelle Coleman was found in the bathroom by the police. She was naked and had been strangled and stabbed in the lower abdomen.

I looked at the photographs and examined the wounds. The poor girl's neck had obvious bruises from strangulation. The stab wound, however, had almost no blood. The knife looked like a hunting knife. It was left in her body and was jammed in right up to the hilt. It was in her extreme lower abdomen just an inch or two above her genitals.

As I reviewed the file, I wrote some questions for myself. My first question was *Why so little blood?* My second and third came after seeing Coleman's hands in some other pictures. *Why no defensive wounds?* and *Anything under the fingernails?*

Michelle Coleman's hands had no cut marks or bruises on them at all. Often, when someone is stabbed to death, he or she tries to block the knife or fight back, and the killer ends up slicing into the victim's hands. It is also common for someone being attacked to scratch the attacker. This can often result in skin or blood under the fingernails, which may provide the DNA profile of the killer.

My last question was answered a few minutes later when I noticed a report from Dr. Randy Young, the recently appointed county coroner. Dr. Young's report showed that he collected material from under the victim's fingernails and sent it to the New York State Police Lab for analysis. I scratched question three off the list.

I paused my review of the file long enough to finish off the chicken and mashed potatoes, as well as the chocolate brownie in the plastic dish. When I was done eating, I realized I had forgotten to bring any paper towels. I should have gotten up for some, but was just too comfortable in my chair. So I used my old T-shirt. Why not? I was supposed to do the laundry soon anyway.

I continued reading the file. I took careful note that the officer in charge of taking fingerprints wrote in his report that "no fingerprints, marks, or smudges were found in the bathroom." This told me that the killer had wiped down the bathroom very carefully. A later report from one of the detectives offered the same conclusion.

Prints were found, however, in the bedroom. A partial right palm print was found on a nightstand near Michelle Coleman's bed. There were also fingerprints found on a jewelry box located on a dresser on the other side of the room and on the windowsill. Police had run the prints through a state database and got a hit. The prints were from the hands of Bob Clancy.

I found the signed statement from Michelle Coleman's neighbor, Clara Brooks, that had been mentioned by DA Worthington. Brooks reported that she was looking out her window and saw a man climbing out of the second-story window of the Coleman home. She claimed the man went out of the window onto a porch roof and then climbed down a maple tree at the side of the house. She immediately called the police. As a result, she never saw how the man left the area. A later report revealed that Clara picked Bob Clancy out of a lineup and identified him as the climber.

I also found the reports detailing the arrest of Bob Clancy. He was arrested at his apartment. A search by detectives uncovered a charm necklace and a gold bracelet that were later identified by Michelle's parents.

There were no statements from Clancy himself. He apparently demanded a lawyer the moment police arrived at his apartment. Under New York law, once a suspect requests an attorney, he is not supposed to be questioned without having that attorney present. Clancy had two prior felonies on his record, so he knew the system very well.

So, just as Rob Worthington had bragged, there were fingerprints and an eyewitness tying Clancy to the murder scene. Clancy had also been found to have the victim's necklace and bracelet in his apartment. They of course came from the same wooden jewelry box that had Clancy's palm print. This was Worthington's open-and-shut case.

I had to admit that things did not look very good for Bob Clancy. Yet, two things continued to gnaw at me. First, why was there not more blood at the scene? A knife had been stuck into the girl's abdomen. The scene ought to be bloody. It appeared the killer had wiped away any fingerprints in the bathroom. Maybe he had cleaned up the blood as well. There were forensic tests to check for blood even after a thorough cleaning. I made a note to ask Dr. Young and the detectives if such a test had been done. The other possibility was that the knife wound had not occurred until after the girl was dead.

This led me to the second thing that bothered me. If the killer took the time to carefully clean the bathroom of prints and possibly blood, why had he not done anything about all the incriminating evidence in the bedroom? There was no indication that Clancy had been interrupted during the cleanup. The police were notified by the nosy neighbor, but she only saw Clancy as he left the house. I added, *Why neat in the bathroom but sloppy in the bedroom?* to my growing list of questions.

Although there was a report from Dr. Young about his observations at the crime scene and his collection of evidence, there was no official coroner's report on the cause of death. I would have to reach out to the doctor to get it. The material under the fingernails was a good possible source of DNA. Since the poor girl was naked, she likely had been raped. If there was any semen recovered, that would be another good source. If the State Police Lab made a DNA match, then it really would be open and shut.

I put the file together again, sat back in my chair, and thought about the case as I drank the rest of my beer. Though I really wanted this case to be over and done with, I kept hearing Bills over and over in my head saying, *My gut is telling me that Clancy is not good for this.*

I thought, *You just might be right, old man.*

I got up and walked back into the house. I took care of the dishes, which consisted of washing a fork and throwing the plastic frozen dinner tray into the trash. I put the Clancy file on my dining room table and went upstairs to my bedroom.

As I undressed and got ready for bed, another voice was ringing in my mind. This time, it was Eddie: *Don't let the fuckers get you down.*

5

The next morning, I was up early. I showered, shaved, and dressed. I chose a charcoal pinstriped suit with a red tie and matching pocket handkerchief.

I grabbed both the Martinez and Clancy files and left for another thrilling day. I drove my Cherokee down the hill and headed toward a small deli called Bonnie's. There, I bought a ham-and-egg bagel and an extra-large coffee with cream and sugar.

By the time I reached the workers' compensation court about twenty minutes later, I had already finished my breakfast sandwich and nearly all of my coffee was gone. I pulled into the lot, parked, and finished the coffee.

I grabbed the Martinez file and walked into the building. I was barely through court security before Annabelle Martinez confronted me. "Mr. Connor, I need to talk to you," she insisted.

"Annabelle," I answered, "I just got here. Go sit down and I will be with you in a few minutes."

I walked past her and into the attorney's room. She was muttering something in Spanish, and I knew I was better off not knowing the translation. Clients are usually jumpy just before appearing before a judge, and often say things to their attorney they later regret.

Twenty minutes later, I left, with Annabelle thanking me profusely. The carrier's medical report had been excluded by the judge and the motion to reduce payments denied. I knew that within the next three months, the carrier would have Annabelle examined again and she would face a brand-new reduction motion. I decided not to tell her just yet. Let her think I was a super lawyer wearing a red cape for a few weeks before she came back to my office all worked up again.

I drove back to my office. I put Annabelle Martinez out of my mind and allowed the Coleman murder to resume center stage. I was still not happy about prosecuting a case again, but found that my focus was more toward the unanswered questions in the case than the painful memories of the past.

I reached Oak Street and drove into the office lot behind the building. There, in my personal parking spot, was a large and very familiar red Dodge Ram.

Dominick "Dom" Bryce was the owner of the offending truck. Dom is not only one of the best investigators I have ever worked with, but also a great friend. He worked for many years in the county sheriff's office, retiring as a detective lieutenant. When I first met him, he was working as an investigator for then DA John Hardy. When Hardy moved up to judge and Rob Worthington became district attorney, Dom immediately put in his papers and retired.

When Senior Investigator Roger Billingsley and Worthington himself asked Dom to stay on with the new administration, Dom looked over at Rob Worthington and said, "Bills, I can't work with that jerk."

As both Dom and Bills tell the story, as Dom turned to leave, Worthington called out, "Why can't you work for me?"

Dom walked over and looked Worthington dead in the eyes.

He then said something that has become legend throughout the county and has made Dom one of my heroes. He said, "Rob, you're a no-good lying fuck, and you've been a no-good lying fuck for thirty years."

I smiled as I thought about that story before parking in the spot next to my own. I grabbed my files off the passenger seat and locked the car. Instead of going into the office, I decided to climb the back steps and go into the apartment above the office.

In addition to storing supplies up there, I also kept extra clothes and personal items in the apartment. I could have just rented out the place for a few extra dollars, but my practice was really not about making big money. My brief time at Wilson, Beckett had netted me more than enough money to live on. At this point in my career, I wanted to help people and fight for legal justice. I can't say I had secured very much justice thus far, but I had helped people, albeit mostly in very small ways.

The practice was making money, but I poured almost all of it back into the office. Casey may not have known it, but her current salary was considerably higher than most other law office managers—secretaries—in the area. She also had no idea that some of the profits had been placed in an account for a considerable Christmas bonus for her.

As for the apartment, it worked very well as a combination of storage space, emergency sleeping quarters, and a place for me to change clothes.

Since there were no more court appearances for the day, I decided to change into business casual, which for me meant that I removed my tie.

Satisfied with my new attire, I went down the interior stairs and into my law office. Casey was at her desk with her head down as she was writing something. Her hair was in a ponytail and she was wearing a white blouse with green intricate designs. Her shirt was long-sleeved, so no tattoos were visible today. As she usually did, she left enough top buttons open to show some cleavage, which was always appreciated by our younger male clients.

Without looking up, Casey said, "Mr. Wonderful is waiting for you in your office."

From within my office, Dom's booming voice echoed, "That's right, baby. In the flesh, though not as nice as your flesh, beautiful."

Without missing a beat or even looking up, Casey fired back, "That's because your flesh is as old as dirt."

I burst out laughing, and Dom yelled back, "You know you love me, beautiful."

"Yeah," Casey answered, finally looking up, "just like I love the chicken pox or leprosy."

"All right," I said, interrupting, "Both of you to neutral corners."

I walked toward my office, stopping right at the doorway. I turned back to Casey and said, "Hold my calls while I meet with this guy."

As I closed the office door behind me, I heard Casey reply, "Better you than me, Connor."

Dom Bryce was sitting on one of the two visitor chairs in my office. He was dressed in a white button-down shirt and blue jeans. His belt had a very large buckle with an eagle and the inscriptions "SECOND AMENDMENT" above and "THE RIGHT TO BEAR ARMS" underneath. To add to his look, he had a Colt 45 revolver in a hip holster and a black cowboy hat on his head. He was wearing brown leather boots, which were clearly visible since his feet were resting on the second visitor's chair that Dom had set up as his own personal footstool.

Dom may have looked like a sidekick in an old country western movie, but he was nobody's fool. He could shoot better than anyone I have ever known and his investigative instincts were second to none. There were few people you could count on in a pinch more than Dom Bryce.

"You comfortable?" I asked sarcastically.

"Better if I had a good beer," he replied with a smile before adding, "but at 9am, it's at least an hour too early."

I sat in my chair and asked, "So, to what do I owe the pleasure, my friend?"

"Well, word has it that you need an investigator," Dom answered. "You ain't gonna solve that big murder case without my help."

"Word gets around," I said. "Hardy call you?"

"Nope, Bills did. Said you could use the help."

"I sure can," I responded.

Before Dom could say anything more, my door opened and Casey came walking in with my favorite coffee mug. I could see the steam rising from the cup. I had just been thinking that I could really go for another cup. She placed it on my desk without a word and then turned for the door.

"Hey beautiful," Dom asked, "nothing for me?"

Without slowing, Casey said, "We're out of Wild Turkey today, old timer."

As I laughed to myself, Dom shot me a look of annoyance. That made it even funnier.

Dom ignored me, took his feet off the second chair, and sat up. He took off his hat and set it on the now-empty chair. "Okay, Connor, what do we have?"

I went over the basic facts of the file. Dom listened without comment until I mentioned the lack of blood and the location of the hunting knife stab wound.

"Let me see those crime scene photos," Dom ordered in a very serious tone. I handed them over and he looked at them intently. He said nothing, but continued to stare at the photos. So I continued with my discussion of the evidence, as well as my list of questions. However, it was clear that he was not listening at all. Then Dom put the pictures down on my desk. "What was the cause of death?" he asked.

"I don't know," I answered. "There is no official coroner's report yet. Just some preliminary reports." I handed those reports to Dom. He scanned them quickly and gave them back to me.

Dom sat there for a minute. He was clearly not happy about something. His eyes seemed far away.

"What is it?" I asked. "Something is really bothering you. Nothing ever fazes you, but you look like you have seen a ghost."

"It's probably nothing," he finally answered.

"Bullshit!" I thundered. "I've known you for a long fucking time. Whatever this is, it is not 'probably nothing.' Talk to me."

Dom paused for a moment and then said, "What's your schedule look like today?"

I was not happy that he was avoiding my question. Finally, I replied, "Let me check," and got up and walked out to Casey's desk. I noticed Dom getting out his cell phone as I did so.

"Casey, everything still clear for today?"

"Yup," she answered, "except for one office appointment at four. A new client named Rebecca Jordan. She insisted on seeing you today."

Hearing that name surprised me. Rebecca Jordan, or Becky Foster as I always knew her, was someone I had not seen in a very long time. Becky and I went to school together from the first grade through high school. We had been close friends, though never anything more. It wasn't that I hadn't been interested. In fact, I had been very interested from the moment I met her, but her boyfriends were usually on the football or wrestling team, and were always at least six feet three inches tall and generally well over 200 pounds. At five foot ten and

175 pounds soaking wet, I just did not make the cut, and had never even tried.

A few years after graduation, Becky married Matt Jordan, the high school's star linebacker. Matt fit the usual profile. He was six feet four and was about 220 pounds even in high school. They had a daughter almost a year later, and named her Taylor. They split up after five years of marriage. Matt was a heavy drinker and was arrested more than once for hitting Becky. Though they got back together once or twice, they eventually divorced about two years ago.

"Connor, you still there?" Casey asked loudly. "You zoned out on me."

"Sorry," I said, "just some old memories. I haven't thought about Becky Foster in a long time."

"Foster? I said Jordan," Casey insisted.

I explained that Foster was Becky's maiden name before asking if she had mentioned what she needed from me.

"No," Casey replied, "just that it was important and she had to see you today."

"Well, I guess I'll find out at four," I said, as I went back to my office. As I entered, Dom was finishing his call. I heard him say, "Okay, doc, I'll be there shortly."

As he put his phone away, I said, "We going somewhere, boss?"

"Yeah," Dom answered as he stood up. "I'll drive."

I followed him out the door. He walked right past Casey without even saying a word. This was beyond unusual. Dom always had something suggestive to say to her. Casey noticed and gave me a surprised look. She seemed almost disappointed. I shrugged.

As I got to the back door, I stopped. I got out my car keys and tossed them to Casey. "Once we leave, would you move my car into my parking space?" I asked.

"Aye, aye, skipper," she answered sarcastically.

By the time I got into the parking lot, Dom had his truck pulled out waiting for me. I hopped into the passenger seat and barely closed the door when Dom took off.

"What the fuck?" I hollered as I tried to get my seat belt on. "Where's the fucking fire?"

Dom didn't answer. I was getting fed up with his silent treatment, so I asked in a very demanding voice, "Where the fuck are we going?"

"We're going to see Dr. Randy Young," Dom said. "We need more information on the cause of death."

I had no argument with that. It was one of the questions I had when I read the file, though it had not bothered me as much as it seemed to almost haunt Dom. The look on his face was intense. Whatever was on his mind, it was clear he was not ready to discuss it.

Nothing more was said during the ride. About ten minutes later, we arrived at Dr. Young's office, which had once been a small farmhouse. The prior owner, like many upstate New York farmers, could not afford the ridiculously high property taxes and went bankrupt. The old house was now converted to a doctor's office on the first floor and Dr. Young's home on the second.

Inside the office, we were greeted by Dr. Young's nurse, Mrs. Wayne. She was in her late fifties, but looked sixty-five easily since her hair had gone completely gray. She was wearing a very traditional nurse's uniform complete with the white hat.

When she heard we needed to speak to Dr. Young about a criminal case, she immediately brought us to his private office. It was a small room with a desk, three chairs, and a filing cabinet. Young's medical school diploma hung on what was otherwise an empty wall.

We each grabbed a seat and waited. About five minutes later, the doctor came in. Dr. Young was just that—young. He was about twenty-nine years old, but barely looked old enough to buy beer. He had bushy, dark-brown hair and was wearing green hospital scrubs.

We all shook hands and Young took a seat behind his desk.

"Doctor," I began, "I'm looking into the murder of Michelle Coleman and I have a few questions."

"I want to know about the cause of death," Dom interrupted rather tersely.

Though I was annoyed at the interruption, I just looked at the doctor waiting for an answer.

"The girl was strangled," Young said.

"What about the stab wound?" I asked.

"It happened after she was dead," Dom announced. It was a statement, not a question.

"The hunting knife was put into the body postmortem," the doctor confirmed.

"That's why there was no blood?" I asked.

"Yes," Young replied, "when someone dies, and the heart stops beating, the blood starts to collect in the lowest part of the body. The Coleman girl was placed on her back after she was strangled. The blood started collecting in the back of her head, shoulders, legs, and back. When that knife was put in, there was no blood because she was already dead."

Now I had another question answered. This one bothered me though. Why would a drunk like Clancy take the girl's clothes and take the time to stab an already dead body?

This sounded like a personal killing or, even worse, a ritualistic murder. Clancy was a drunk and a burglar, but there was no indication of anything more sinister in his background. Either Clancy was more than just a local drunk and drug addict, or maybe the murderer was someone else.

I still had other unanswered questions, so I asked, "What about the fingernail scrapings?"

"We don't have them back yet. They were sent to the state police lab for analysis, along with a sample from the suspect." Young said, "We should have the results back any day now."

"Was there any semen recovered?"

"No," came the answer immediately, but it was not Dr. Young speaking. It had been Dom. Both the doctor and I looked at him in surprise.

"How do you know that?" I asked. I was really losing my patience.

Dom let out a slow breath before answering in a stoic, almost emotionless voice. "There isn't going to be any signs of rape or sex." Then, he slowly stood up and walked out of the office without saying a word.

I wanted to go after Dom, but I needed first to find out if he was right. I turned back to Dr. Young. "Well?" I asked.

"You heard the man," Young replied. "The Coleman girl was not raped or sexually assaulted. Her killer strangled her to death, stripped her, and then plunged the knife into her after she was already dead."

Now I was almost certain that Clancy was not the killer. But Dom knew something more. I thanked the doctor for his time and told him I would be in touch.

The doctor asked me to wait for a moment. He walked to his filing cabinet and took out a small folder. "These are copies of all my reports, including the official determination of cause of death." I took the file and headed out.

When I got outside, I found Dom sitting in the open tailgate of his truck. He was smoking a cigarette and staring straight ahead. His face was absolutely expressionless.

When he did not say anything more, I finally had enough. "Okay, cut the cloak-and-dagger shit!" I yelled. "You already knew that the knife wound was postmortem and that she had not been raped. I want to know how you knew all of that."

"I didn't know for sure," Dom finally answered, "I just suspected."

"Suspected what?" I demanded. "You are not answering my question. I want to know how you knew there would be no evidence of rape."

Dom seemed to consider his response for a long time before he finally answered, "Because there never was all the other times that monster killed."

6

After dropping his bombshell, Dom refused to say anything more. The entire ride back to my office, I badgered him, screamed at him, and all but threatened to kill him. He still would not provide an answer.

When he stopped in front of my office, he finally spoke. "Connor, I know this killer. I'll come by your house tonight at nine o'clock with as much beer as we can drink and as many answers as I can possibly give you."

I stared at him in disbelief. I could not understand why he was being so secretive. Yet, in all the years I have known him, he never once lied to me. I decided to give him the benefit of the doubt. "All right, boss," I said, as I got out of his truck. "Nine o'clock. But I am not waiting one minute more. You hear?"

Dom just nodded. I shut the door and he took off immediately.

I watched until he was out of sight, and then went inside. I was dying to know what could bother Dom Bryce this much, but knew I was not going to learn anything until nine o'clock tonight.

I spent the next hour in my office with the door closed,

reviewing all the medical documents Dr. Young had given me. In addition to his autopsy report and official cause of death declaration, there were also details on some of the forensic evidence.

A preliminary review of the fingernail scrapings suggested blood and possibly skin tissue. This made it all the more likely that the State Police Lab would be able to obtain a DNA profile of Michelle Coleman's killer. This would allow for a definitive inclusion or exclusion of Bob Clancy, though I was pretty sure of his innocence.

I also took another look at the district attorney's file to see if I had missed anything. About halfway through that file, my intercom buzzed. I reached over and hit the button without looking away from the folder. "What is it, Casey?"

"Ray Stanton for you on line one, Connor."

Ray Stanton is an attorney with the public defender's office. I remembered from my file that he had been assigned to defend Bob Clancy. I am sure he was just as thrilled to be on this case as I was.

Stanton had been with the public defender's office for nearly twenty years. He was an excellent trial attorney, though his reputation was that he hated doing trials and always looked for a plea bargain.

In my stint with the district attorney's office, I had many cases with Ray. He was always easy to deal with. The biggest problem was looking at him with a straight face. Ray Stanton was bald except for some thin gray hair on the sides of his head. Unfortunately, he had never learned to accept it. Rather than be an openly bald man, he instead chose to wear a truly horrible toupee.

His wig was much darker than his remaining hair. The resulting look was thin gray on the sides and thick dark brown on top. One old lady who once saw him in court was overheard to declare that the toupee looked like a throw rug on a hardwood floor.

Obviously, Toupee Ray (as he was called) must have heard about my assignment and was looking to make a deal. The problem was I was not ready to make an offer yet. I took the call anyway. "Hello, Ray. I assume you are calling to see about a deal?" I asked.

"Actually, Connor, I'm not," Ray answered. "I am just letting you know that my client will not accept any deals on this. He insists he did not kill that girl."

I was only mildly surprised by this development. How could I expect his client to confess to murder when I was not at all certain that he had even done it? "I am not making any offers yet," I said. "I just got the case yesterday and I'm looking through the evidence. I would like to talk with your client, though."

Ray laughed. "I'm sure you would, pal, but you know I can't—"

"Look, Ray," I interrupted, "I'm going to give it to you straight. I don't think your guy killed her."

"Then why is my guy still in jail?" Ray thundered in feigned indignation. "If you have evidence that exonerates my client, you know you have to turn it over."

"Cool your jets, counselor," I answered. "I didn't say your client was innocent. I have no doubt that Clancy broke into the house and committed burglary. With his record, that's enough for another trip to the state country club. I'm just not sure he committed murder."

"Connor, if you're offering a plea to just the burglary, then maybe we can make a deal. Just let me talk—"

"No, Ray. Don't get ahead of yourself," I cautioned. "I should have something for you in a day or two. When I have something, I'll call you."

We talked for a few minutes more. Ray kept pushing for

more information and I kept stalling him. Finally, we finished the call and I went back to reading the file.

I spent the rest of the afternoon reviewing police reports and making some phone calls. I called the two police officers who first arrived at the murder scene to check on some details. They offered nothing beyond their reports, which was rather frustrating.

Then I called the state police lab to see when the DNA test results would be ready. I was surprised to learn from the now aggravated lab technician that Dom Bryce had already called him about it. The tech assured me that he would email me the results no later than ten o'clock tomorrow morning. I apologized for pestering him and thanked him for his very prompt work.

Tonight at nine o'clock, I was going to get some answers out of Dom Bryce no matter what. I was just imagining some of the creative ways I would beat the truth out of him when there was a knock at the door.

I got up and pulled open the door expecting to see Casey. Instead, Becky Foster stood before me.

She looked very much as I remembered her from high school. She was about five feet four inches tall with long blonde hair. Her eyes were hazel-brown and she was wearing blue jeans and a long yellow T-shirt that matched her hair.

"Hi, Connor," she said with a smile as bright as her eyes.

"Becky," I said almost stupidly before giving her a rather awkward hug. "It's nice to see you again."

There was palpable silence. Becky and I had spent many hours together in school, yet now I could not seem to find any words. The silence was mercifully broken when Becky asked if she could sit down.

I pointed her to one of the chairs and took a seat behind my desk. "So, what brings you to see me?" I asked. Better to get to the point of her visit than allow that silence to return.

Becky frowned. "My ex-husband."

"Ah, the famous linebacker," I offered. "You already divorced him. What do you need me to do?"

Becky opened her purse and pulled out some papers. I could tell by the blue backer paper that they were legal documents. She handed them to me and I took a look. It was a restraining order issued against Matt Jordan by the Linton County Family Court. It had the usual language requiring Matt to not come closer than one hundred feet to Becky or her home, business, etc. It also prevented contact by phone or in writing.

When I finished reading it, I looked up at Becky. "Looks like a standard stay-away order," I said.

Becky looked very uncomfortable for a moment. "Well," she said, "Matt keeps driving by my house every night. He never comes to the door. He just sits in his old truck and smokes and drinks beer. He stays there for two to three hours at a time just watching."

Sounds like a typical jackass jock who peaked in high school, I thought. "Have you called the police?" I asked, trying not to show my disgust.

"Yes, but Matt's cousin works for the sheriff, so they don't do anything. They come by, talk to him, and he just laughs."

"This kind of thing sometimes happens in small rural communities like Rockfield," I said, "but I can make sure different officers handle your calls."

I had a pretty good idea who Matt's cousin was. I made a mental note to have Dom Bryce use his significant contacts with the sheriff's office to make sure that Matt's cousin was moved to a different work shift. Maybe a few weeks of cleaning the inmate toilets would change his attitude.

Becky stared at me for a long moment without speaking. Tears began to slide down her cheeks. I was surprised by how much that bothered me. I grabbed a box of tissues from my desk and handed it to her.

She pulled out a tissue, dabbed her eyes, and sniffed loudly before speaking again. "I have a court date in a few weeks," she said, "but what am I going to do until then? He's there every night right after he gets off work."

Again, the tears flowed silently. She looked down at the floor. When she spoke again, she did so without looking up. "I am so scared of him, Connor. He has hit me so many times. One time, he even pulled a gun on me. I just want him to stop and leave me alone." Her voice trailed off as her tears continued. She looked like she was reliving memories of one of Matt's many beatings.

I could feel my anger growing rapidly. It was like liquid fire pulsing throughout my body. Becky was always very sweet to everyone she met. She always went out of her way for people. Yet, she had ended up with a miserable lowlife whose best years were behind him before the age of twenty-five.

"He just won't leave me alone," Becky continued. "He threatens anyone I even try dating. He shows up at my house whenever he feels like it."

Becky's voice was quivering as she spoke. She was trying very hard not to let the pain within her overpower her. It appeared to me that she was slowly losing that battle.

"He told me once that I am his woman and that he owns me," Becky croaked through her tears and stifled sobs.

I tried to keep my red-hot rage from exploding. I decided then and there that I was going to handle this problem one way or the other.

"Becky," I said firmly in a tone that was louder than I intended. She looked up quickly, obviously startled at my volume.

I took a slow breath and made sure to speak in a much softer tone. "Where does Matt work?"

"He's a mechanic at Tony's Garage," she replied.

I knew the place. It was only five or six blocks from my office.

I tried to smile reassuringly. "You just leave it to me. I will make him stop."

She looked at me questioningly. "What are you going to do, Connor?"

I did not want to tell her. In truth, I wasn't really sure myself. I only knew that Matt Jordan was tormenting her and I was going to put an end to it.

"Don't worry about that," I answered. "You just leave it to me."

She did not look thrilled with my answer. "Connor," she said accusingly, "what are you planning to—"

"Becky," I interrupted, "you came to me for help, right?"

"Yes," she answered haltingly.

"Then trust me. I know what I'm doing," I said. I hoped she would accept my words, just as I also hoped that I really did know what I was doing.

She obviously decided not to challenge me further. Instead, she smiled through the remnants of her tears and softly said, "Thank you."

We spoke for another five or ten minutes just sort of catching up. Finally, as she stood to leave, Becky looked serious. "Connor, I don't have a lot of money, but if you will let me make monthly payments on your attorney fee, I can—"

I held up my hand to stop her. "Don't worry about my fee right now," I said. "We'll talk about that another time."

The look on her face showed amusement, surprise, and something else I could not quite identify. "I want to pay you for your time, Mr. Phelan," she said, both firmly and almost whimsically.

I smiled and walked out from behind my desk. "We'll work

something out, Miss Foster," I answered, trying to mimic the same tone.

Without another word and without acknowledging that I had used her maiden name, Becky stepped toward me and hugged me again. This hug was not awkward and seemed to last significantly longer than the first. I was very conscious of the softness of her hair, the feel of her body, and the subtle sweetness of her perfume.

After the hug, we said our goodbyes and Becky left. I stood in my office and it took only a few moments for my simmering fury to return. It was understandably directed at Matt Jordan. If I was being really honest, a lot of the anger was directed at myself, though I was not exactly sure why. I thought about it for a few seconds, but decided not to be honest, at least not this night.

7

I left the office at about half past four. I wanted to make sure I could get to Tony's Garage before closing time. It probably would have been better to wait before speaking with Matt Jordan; nonetheless, I drove directly there.

Tony's Garage was in a small brick building. There was a customer entrance on the far left side and two garage bays on the right. Since I was not there to get my oil changed, I walked right into the first bay. Though there were two distinct doors, the inside was just one large room that had been divided into separate workspaces, complete with car lifts and various tools and devices. Between the two was a large pile of metal hubcaps from different types of cars. The pile was organized to look like a display or memorial.

Matt Jordan was a few feet in front of me looking down into the open hood of a Chevrolet.

"Matt," I announced in a voice that made it clear I was not going to wait.

He looked up. Jordan looked somewhat different than he had in high school. For starters, he was at least forty or fifty pounds heavier and it looked like most of the weight was in his round stomach. He still looked strong and had large muscles in his arms and neck. His once-thick hair was considerably thinner and the beginnings of male-pattern baldness were visible under an oily old ball cap that covered only a portion of his head.

"Well, if it ain't the big hotshot lawyer," Matt said with a sneer. He put down the wrench he had been using, wiped his hands on his filthy work shirt, and stepped toward me. He was much bigger than me, but I was not about to back down from him. We glared at each other for a moment, neither giving an inch.

"So," the big man asked, "what the fuck do you want?"

"Stay away from Becky," I commanded, trying to sound tough.

Matt just laughed. "And if I don't?" he asked, talking another half step toward me.

"For starters, you go to jail," I said without flinching.

"Go ahead and call the cops," he sneered. "They ain't gonna do shit."

Now I smiled. "Ah, yes, your cousin at the sheriff's office," I said. "I made a few phone calls and he is being reassigned to the midnight shift inside the jail. He's going to be much too busy shoveling shit to help you."

I had not actually made the calls yet, but was very confident in Dom's ability to get the transfer done. Plus, the big dope did not know that anyway.

Matt's face immediately flushed. I glanced down to see his hands. If he threw one of those giant fists at me, I had to be ready. Matt seemed to be struggling to think. It was obviously not his forte.

Finally, he said, "I'll see Becky whenever I want. She's my woman and ain't you or no court gonna say otherwise."

To this point, I had been very controlled. When I heard his words, I remembered Becky crying in my office and became incensed to the point that I could hear my pulse pounding in my ears.

"You listen to me, and you listen good, you no-good son of a bitch," I growled. "If I ever find out that you so much as lay a finger on her, jail will be the least of your worries."

He reached up with his right hand, grabbed my suit lapel, and yanked me toward him. I stepped forward as he pulled and smacked him in the chin with a right uppercut. His head snapped up with the blow. In that moment, I grabbed his hand that was still holding my lapel. As I grabbed it, I placed my thumb on the knuckle of his left ring finger. I pressed hard on Matt's hand, applying a painful wristlock, and made sure his hand was pressed against my chest. Then I stepped back with my left foot and completely pivoted my body. This movement, along with the wristlock, caused Matt to flip right over my right hip and land with a thud on the concrete floor.

It also caused my suit jacket to tear. I did not have time, however, to check the damage.

Matt was stunned for just a second. He yanked his hand and arm away, rolled over, and got to his feet. He grabbed the large wrench he had been working with and came at me, swinging it. I ducked under his attack and punched him as hard as I could in the ribs.

Matt took a small step back after the punch. I backed away, trying to give myself more room to maneuver. Matt followed me. I kept backing up until I found myself trapped with Matt in front of me and the odd-looking hubcap display behind me.

Matt saw that I had nowhere to go. He let out a growl and charged at me with the wrench, trying to hit me on top of my head. As he did, I stepped forward with my right foot. I blocked his attack by grabbing his wrist with my left hand and pulling him forward, allowing his own momentum to continue. I slipped underneath him and flung him with a right-side shoulder throw.

Matt crashed into the pile of hubcaps. The display collapsed and the metal disks went flying. As they landed on the floor, the sound echoed throughout the garage. It made one hell of a racket.

Matt lay on the floor with the wind knocked out of him. Before he could get up, I walked over and stepped on his throat. I put enough pressure and weight on him to cause considerable pain, but not enough to cause permanent damage. I had his undivided attention.

"If you come near Becky again," I said, "you'll end up in jail or in the hospital or both."

I added slightly more pressure on his throat to make my point. I held it only for a moment before releasing his neck and walking away. Two other people from the garage had obviously heard the noise and came to check on Matt. I walked right past them and out of the bay door. I went straight to my Grand Cherokee and drove off.

I went a few blocks and then circled back. Becky had said that Matt always went to her house right after work. I decided to make sure he didn't.

I parked down the street from Tony's Garage and waited. About ten or fifteen minutes later, Matt Jordan walked out of the garage and got into a 1988 Ford F-150 pickup that had once been white. Now it was faded, badly rusted, and covered with dirt and mud. The truck was thirty years old and looked it. He started the engine and the loud roar made it clear that his muffler was shot. Isn't it strange that mechanics always drive the biggest pieces of junk?

He drove out of the parking lot and I followed him from a distance. I had seen private detectives and policemen on television tailing a suspect many times. I had never done it myself, so I had no idea how to do it. I just kept back and tried to drive casual.

Matt drove straight to a local bar called Sully's. The place was barely a hole in the wall and had a reputation of being very tough. I pulled over to the side of the road, and watched him park his car and walk in. I waited almost an hour, but Matt did not return.

I left and drove over to Becky's home. She lived in a small house on a dead-end street. I parked just before the turnoff to her road and waited. If Matt Jordan was coming, he had to drive right past me.

I waited for almost ninety minutes. Jordan's ugly truck never appeared. Satisfied that he was not going to bother Becky this night, I started my car and headed home.

The first thing I did when I got home was change my clothes. Though Jordan had not landed a single punch, he had destroyed my suit. A jagged tear now decorated the entire left side of the jacket near the lapel. No amount of tailoring was going to save it. I threw the suit into the trash can and changed into jeans and a T-shirt.

I went down to the kitchen and prepared another gourmet meal. Tonight was the leftover pizza I had declined the night before. As it warmed in the microwave, I got myself a cold beer. When the microwave dinged, I got my food, took it and the beer into the living room, and ate my dinner while watching the nightly news.

After my feast, I must have dozed off. I was awakened by the ringing of my doorbell. As I headed toward the door, I looked at the clock and saw it was five minutes to nine. I was therefore not surprised that Dom Bryce was the one ringing the bell.

True to his word, he brought with him two six-packs of beer, as well as four large boxes of files. I helped him bring it all into the dining room. Once there, we each opened a beer and sat down.

It seemed like an eternity before Dom finally spoke. He took a large drag on the beer and then said, "You ever hear of the Rockfield Strangler?"

I had. The Rockfield Strangler had killed three women in the late 1990s and nearly killed a fourth. Then he mysteriously stopped and was never heard from again.

"Yeah," I answered, "but that was about twenty years ago when I was away in college. You don't actually think the Strangler killed Michelle Coleman, do you?"

Despite my dismissive tone, Dom's face did not change expression. He kept the same hard and determined look that he had from the moment he arrived.

"I don't think he did it," Dom replied defiantly. "I know damn fucking well he did."

My head was now starting to spin and it was not the beer causing it. For the life of me, I could not understand how Dom could offer such a fantastic story. "I know Coleman was strangled," I said, "but that doesn't mean a ghost from twenty years ago is the killer."

Dom reached into one of the boxes and took out several folders. He handed them to me and said in a voice barely above a whisper, "As you may remember from your days as a prosecutor, investigators always hold back certain significant facts."

"Sure," I answered, "so if a suspect knows about them, it is a sign of guilt."

"That's right," Dom continued. "We never released to the media or to anyone that in every murder committed by that scumbag, a hunting knife was stabbed into each woman right above her pussy and it was always done after death. He never raped the women. He choked them to death, stripped them, and stuck a big fucking knife into them."

As he said this, I opened the first folder. The tab identified the folder as "Photos—Kim Garrett Murder Scene." Inside were several old-style color photographs. I looked at the top one. It showed a young woman, maybe twenty-one or twenty-two years old, lying naked in the back seat of a car. A large hunting knife protruded from her lower abdomen. I had to admit that it looked a lot like the Coleman murder scene.

I looked back at Dom. "It is similar," I admitted, "but I—"

"No," Dom interrupted forcefully, "it is the same fucking guy. There's no doubt in my mind. Every one of those folders will show the same thing. A dead girl choked to death with a great big knife stuck in her afterwards."

We stared at each other for a moment before Dom continued.

"I was the chief investigator on these cases. I worked it for years. We could never quite get a suspect. We came close once, but never got him. Then the sucker just disappeared without a trace. We tried hospitals, prisons, everything we could think of to explain why he just stopped. Nothing."

As Dom looked away thinking about the past, it suddenly dawned on me. Every detective has that one unsolved case that haunts him even after retirement. This was Dom's case, his obsession from his days as a detective.

"Look," I said, bringing Dom back to the present, "I'm expecting DNA results tomorrow, which will tell us one way or the other if Clancy was the killer. Assuming he's cleared, how are we going to connect this new murder to the Rockfield Strangler killings? How will we prove it is not a copycat killer?"

"I've already taken care of that," Dom answered immediately.

I did not like the sound of that. Bryce had already called the state police lab. He obviously had taken some other action without telling me.

"What did you do?" I asked suspiciously.

Dom took in a big breath before answering. "I sent another DNA profile to the lab tech for comparison."

"Whose profile?" I demanded. I was getting really annoyed at not being kept in the loop.

"The Strangler's second victim was a hooker named Darlene Johnson," Dom said. "When she was being choked, she scratched the bastard. We recovered a small amount of blood under her fingernails and got a DNA profile. We just never found a suspect that matched it."

Now I realized what he had done. "So, without even saying one word to me about it," I accused, "you took it upon yourself to send that profile to the lab to compare with the sample from the Coleman killing?"

"Yeah," Dom answered flatly.

This was the final straw. I could not have my investigator running rogue any further. I had to put a stop to it. "Let's get something clear right now, cowboy," I said in an angry voice, "this is my fucking case now, not yours. From this moment on, when it comes to my case, you do not do anything without checking with me first, or I get myself a brand-new investigator. You don't even wipe your ass without my permission, you got it?"

Dom smiled slightly before saying, "Connor, I want this fucking guy more than I have ever wanted any other scumbag."

I started to respond, but he continued. "You're right. I'm working for you on this one. You're the boss."

I think Dom knew I had absolutely no intention of getting a new investigator. He also knew that he had overstepped by not telling me what he had done. Yet, I think we also both knew that while he had not specifically said so, this was as close as Dom would ever come to an apology. In truth, I didn't need one.

For twenty years, this case had burned a hole in Dom's gut. Now he believed the killer was back and he was not going to let him escape again. I understood very well how memories of the past can hold onto your heart and soul without compassion or pity.

"Just run things by me before you go off half-cocked," I said, before grabbing two beers and handing one to Dom. I held up my beer in a silent toast. He clinked his bottle against mine. We had known each for enough years that words were not necessary. This was our way of declaring the argument over.

We continued over the course of the evening to drink beer and go over the files from the Rockfield Strangler murders. Tomorrow morning, we would both get an email with the lab results. The lab report would convict or exonerate Clancy. It might also confirm the return of a vicious and evil killer.

8

At 9am the following morning, I was in my office reviewing the files Dom had dropped off the night before. The police reports, lab reports, and photographs told a very disturbing story of the Strangler's murderous rampage in the late 1990s.

On Saturday, 27 February, 1999, he killed his first victim. She was Kim Garrett, a twenty-two-year-old waitress who worked in a twenty-four-hour diner on the outskirts of town. At 6am, her boss saw her car still in the lot, looked inside and found Garrett dead in the back seat. Police speculated that her killer had been waiting for her after she got off work around two in the morning.

Her killer choked her to death. After she was dead, he stripped off her clothes, pulled out a hunting knife, and stuck it into her abdomen. He then took her clothes with him and left. He had not sexually abused or raped her.

There was almost no forensic evidence found. No fibers were found in and around the bruises on the woman's neck. She had not been strangled manually with the use of a cord or ligature. Based on the bruising, he had not used his hands. Likely, he had wrapped his entire arm around her neck and choked her with his forearm.

Almost two months later, on Sunday, 18 April, 1999, an old man was walking his dog through the woods when he found the body of Darlene Johnson. She was a thirty-four-year-old prostitute and was found in almost the same condition as Kim Garrett. When found, it appeared that she had been dead for about two days.

The working police theory was that her killer picked her up and made a deal for sex. They drove to the wooded area where she was found, and he strangled her, stripped her, and so forth. There was no sign of rape or sexual abuse. Whatever the real motive, it was not about sex.

Just as Dom had said, there were lab reports showing the DNA profile obtained from the small amount of blood found under Darlene's fingernails. She had scratched her attacker during the assault. It was the only piece of forensic evidence from any of the crime scenes.

On 21 November, 1999, the body of seventeen-year-old Susanna Hoskins was found lying by a creek in the same condition as the other victims.

Police determined that Susanna had told her parents she was going bowling the night before with her friend, Hillary Contini. Unbeknownst to Mom and Dad, she planned instead to first secretly meet her boyfriend, Tyrone Anderson. Her parents objected to the relationship because Tyrone was black and had forbidden her to continue seeing him. This only intensified the teenager's desire for her boyfriend.

After meeting with Tyrone, Hoskins planned to walk to the bowling alley and meet Contini. The plan was then to go and stay at Hillary's house. When the bowling alley closed and Susanna had not appeared, Contini called the missing girl's parents, hoping her friend had returned home. When she found out that her friend was not at home, she panicked and confessed the whole affair. The now frightened and worried parents immediately called the police. About six hours later, police made the gruesome discovery of the body.

Unlike the other two killings, evidence technicians found signs of sexual activity, including semen. Police initially suspected Tyrone to be the killer and questioned him at length. He freely admitted meeting Susanna that night and having sex with her. He denied killing her.

Local newspapers ran two or three stories suggesting Anderson's guilt as a jilted lover. A few weeks later, the State Police Lab matched the DNA from the semen to Tyrone Anderson. However, he did not match the DNA taken from the blood found under Darlene Johnson's fingernails. He was eventually cleared as a suspect.

Nearly seven months later, on Saturday, 17 June, 2000, seventeen-year-old Amy Allen was out with her friends at a local drive-in. After the movie, she had her friend, Heather Newman, drop her off two blocks from her house. (She was past curfew and did not want to be heard.)

After Heather drove off, Amy was about a block away from home when she was attacked. A stranger came from behind, grabbed her, and started choking her. She struggled and would have died, but two guys (Terry Whitlock and his brother Jerry) happened to be driving by and saw what was happening. They stopped their car, got out, and ran toward Amy and her would-be killer.

The attacker released his chokehold and ran off. Amy and the Whitlocks gave a basic description of the attacker. He was about six feet tall and slender, with brown hair, and wearing a dark jean jacket. One of the Whitlock brothers claimed to have seen a large knife in a sheath attached to the man's belt.

Police artists released a sketch based on that description, though it was not very specific. In the files was an article from the *Rockfield Tribune* describing the attack complete with the drawing.

It was presumed that Amy's assailant was the elusive Rockfield Strangler. Though there was no proof other than the method of attack, investigators seemed certain that Allen had almost been his fourth victim.

There were no other known attacks, though there was some more recent information about Amy Allen. There were criminal arrest reports showing she was arrested twice for possession of controlled substances and a news clipping from about a year earlier containing her obituary. It seems she never fully recovered from her attack. She turned to drugs and died from an overdose. The obituary also mentioned her surviving husband, Jason Moore. They had no children.

I knew Jason Moore. I had prosecuted him on more than one occasion back in the day. He was a hardcore drug user. He was likely the source of the very drugs that took his wife's life.

Then it occurred to me that if the Rockfield Strangler had indeed started killing again, the recent death of the only person known to have survived his attack was probably not a coincidence. Could he have killed her? Or had she really died from a random drug overdose and now the homicidal maniac felt free to kill once more?

I was getting ahead of myself. There was no proof yet of the Strangler's return. No sense worrying about these scenarios yet.

I put the reports I had been reading back into their folder and set it down on my desk. I went and got my third cup of coffee. My mind was racing as I considered the possibilities. Could the case assigned to me by Judge Hardy really be part of the return of a serial killer who had been dormant for nearly two decades?

If it was, the media would have a field day. It would be the biggest story perhaps in Rockfield's history. I found myself mentally cursing out Judge Hardy. My first prosecution in almost ten years and look what it might become: a damn circus.

I tried for the next hour or so to work on some of my other files. It proved to be nearly impossible. I would read a paragraph or two before my thoughts went back to the murder of Michelle Coleman and the nameless monster who might have resumed his killing spree.

Just before ten o'clock, Dom arrived. Casey announced his arrival, but without the usual sarcastic comment. I had told her everything that was happening. She was too young to remember much about the killing spree from the late 1990s, but understood the gravity of the situation. If this whole thing turned into a huge shitstorm, she would be the one initially taking all the calls and dealing with the walk-ins looking for information.

In her usual way, she had announced that she was not afraid. She boasted that if the Strangler came into the office, she would stab him with her scissors. It was the type of remark she made every once in a while if a client made idle threats. It was one of her ways of dealing with stress and anxiety.

This was different. Despite her tough act, I could see the fear in her eyes. It was really the first time any of my cases had ever done that to her. I hoped it would not make her consider quitting her job. I would understand if she did, but the office would not be the same without her. I considered her more than just an employee. She was like a crazy kid sister to me.

Dom was also not his usual jovial self. He was dressed as he always was, complete with hat, cowboy boots, and Colt 45 revolver. His mood was serious and almost somber. He had made it clear to me last night when we drank and talked that over the years, memories and regrets from this investigation often kept him awake at night. He would retrace the steps he had taken and evidence he had uncovered, just hoping he might have that Perry Mason moment when he would suddenly learn the identity of his quarry. It was an itch he had never been able to scratch.

He sat in one of my visitor chairs sipping his coffee, seemingly lost in thought. Periodically, he checked his cell phone looking for the email from the state lab. It was like waiting for water to boil.

Casey, meanwhile, was doing paperwork. She would stop every now and then and stare into space. I had never seen my office this quiet. It was like a damn tomb. The silence was broken when both Dom's and my cell phone chimed at nearly the same time.

I looked at the screen and saw that the email we had been waiting for had finally arrived. I opened the two files attached to the email. The first was a comparison of the saliva swab taken from Bob Clancy and the material taken from under Michelle Coleman's fingernails. I scanned the report until I got the conclusions. Bob Clancy was excluded. This meant that he was not the man Coleman scratched and thus not the killer.

My stomach tightened as I began to read the second file. It was a comparison between the material taken from under Michelle Coleman's fingernails and what was believed to be the DNA profile of the so-called Rockfield Strangler.

As I skipped to the conclusion and began to read it, Dom stood up. Without a word, he walked out of my office and over to Casey's desk. He talked with her quietly. I could not hear the conversation, but when I saw the look on Casey's face, I did not have to finish reading the report. I knew what it was going to say. I read it anyway and it confirmed what I already assumed. It was a match. After almost twenty years, the Rockfield Strangler was back.

As the impact of the report settled on me, I found that I was not afraid. I could feel my blood pulsing through my chest, but it was not from fear or rage. It was excitement. A few moments ago, I was internally cursing and condemning Judge Hardy for giving me this case. Now I actually was almost happy that he did. The rush of a good investigation was something I had not felt for quite some time.

The Rockfield Strangler was a case that had been discussed on occasion when I was a prosecutor. Then DA Hardy always kept a handful of files of unsolved cases in his office. Some were very old and others were ongoing. Periodically, when it got slow, he would give one of the files to me or to one of the other prosecutors. "Take a look and see what you think," he would always say. "Maybe you'll be a hero and solve it."

He had never given me the Strangler case. I am not even sure if that was one of the files Hardy kept in his desk. The only case he ever gave me was an ongoing series of burglaries. Someone kept breaking into people's homes on Sunday mornings and stealing anything he could.

I worked that file for nearly a month and became preoccupied with it. I nicknamed the suspect "The Mass Intruder" because he always struck on Sundays between nine in the morning and noon when most people in Rockfield were at church. It was that very pattern that eventually resulted in his capture.

I had decided to see if there were any other patterns to the crimes. When I did a detailed review of all the people who had been robbed, I discovered that all of them were Catholic. There were only two Catholic churches in Rockfield, but all the victims went to St. Michael's. The regular masses for Sundays there were at 10am and 11am. A few phone calls later and I had narrowed it down even more. All the victims not only attended St. Michael's, but also attended the 10am Mass.

Within a week, I had coordinated with the Rockfield Police and obtained the names of all the usual attendees at that Mass. Those who had not yet been robbed were placed on a list of likely targets. Undercover police officers were assigned to watch each of the homes of those on the list the following Sunday. I was with one of the sergeants in his car watching a home when a call came over the radio that an arrest had been made.

The "Mass Intruder" turned out to be an eighteen-year-old punk named Tom Dyer. Dyer had once been an altar boy at St. Michael's and still occasionally attended Mass. He had observed all the faithful attendees at the church and then robbed them while they prayed. He had been caught in the act and readily confessed to all the thefts.

I remembered the next Monday when I brought that file back to Hardy and proclaimed it solved. I was pleased when he announced me the hero of the day, but disappointed that he had not handed me another unsolved mystery. It had been over ten years, but now I realized that Hardy had finally given me another one. I understood without having to really ponder it that I was going solve this latest mystery come hell or high water.

I came out of my thoughts when both Dom and Casey walked into my office. I told them to grab a seat.

"Now that we know what we're dealing with," I said, "we have to make sure we are all on the same page."

They both stared at me without saying anything. It was rare that I could speak without one of them interrupting.

"The first thing we have to do is get Bob Clancy into court and have the murder charge dismissed. We can do that this afternoon."

"Connor, wait a minute," Dom chimed in. "You aren't seriously going to announce the return of the Strangler in open court, are you?"

"Of course not," I replied, "I'm not going to mention the report linking him. I'm only going to release the first report that clears Clancy. I'll have the murder charge dismissed, but the burglary and possession of stolen property charges will remain. I will need Clancy to testify about what he saw in that house when he broke in. He might have seen something important. To get that, I will have to make a deal with old Toupee Ray."

Casey snickered. She always enjoyed hearing about Ray Stanton. The first time she had met him, tears had run down her face as she tried desperately not to laugh at his outrageous hairpiece. Just the mere mention of his name always got a reaction.

"Sorry," she said, after realizing her snicker had been heard.

"There is to be no mention to anyone that we are dealing with the Rockfield Strangler," I continued. "As long as he doesn't know we are onto him, we have the advantage. I want to keep that advantage as long as we possibly can."

"What about the calls from the press?" Casey asked. "Once Clancy is cleared, there will be questions."

"That will be easy," I said. "You just tell any reporters who call or stop by that you have no comment. Then say, 'All statements regarding this matter will come from Mr. Phelan himself.'"

Casey's eyes went wide and a slight smile crossed her face. "Mr. Phelan?" she said sarcastically. "Not Connor, but Mr. Phelan?" Her smile widened. "How about I say that all questions must be addressed to the Grand High Special Prosecutor, Mr. Connor Phelan?"

"I think that Mr. Phelan will do just fine, Casey," I responded.

"Wise ass," Dom interjected, himself now starting to smile.

Casey addressed Dom. "Did you say something, Mr. Wonderful?"

"Now look here, little girl," Dom responded sternly.

I sat on my desk and watched as the two of them started squabbling back and forth. Although we had a lot of work to do and I should have broken it up, I decided to just let them bicker for a few minutes. It was as close to normal as my office was probably going to be for the next few weeks.

9

The balance of the morning was spent making arrangements for an afternoon court appearance. Casey called Judge Hardy's chambers to request that Bob Clancy be transported from jail, while I called Toupee Ray.

Ray could just sense that a plea bargain was in the air.

"What are you offering, Connor?" he kept asking.

I assured him over and over again that there was going to be a deal placed on the table, but it would be done in open court. This did not satisfy Ray, but there was nothing he could really do about it. He was still pressing me for information when I told him I had another appointment and disconnected.

Casey hung up her phone a few minutes later. "Old Iron Girdle says that Clancy will be there by 12:45 and the judge will take the bench at one," she hollered from her chair. "Old Iron Girdle" was her usual nickname for Ethel Bollenbacher. It was a little cruel, but it definitely fit. The first time I heard Casey use that nickname, I was drinking coffee and damn near choked.

Dom had left the office shortly after the lab report arrived. Since he would be appearing with me in court, he needed to change into a suit. As he left, I made sure to remind him to wear a proper tie. I knew if I didn't, there was a better than fifty-fifty chance he would show up wearing a western bolo tie.

With the judge and defense counsel contacted, I now started reworking my case file. I printed out several copies of the lab reports. I placed the papers linking the Strangler murders in a manila folder and labeled it "Lab Report—DNA Link."

The copies of the report clearing Clancy of the Coleman murder were placed in a separate folder and labeled "Brady Material."

Brady material is evidence or information that might exonerate a charged defendant. Back in 1963, in a case called *Brady v. Maryland*, the Supreme Court ruled that prosecutors must turn over exculpatory evidence or information to a defendant prior to trial. Failure to do so is misconduct and can lead to ethical sanctions and, in some cases, dismissal of charges. I was going to give Ray Stanton and Judge Hardy copies of this report at the hearing.

I was careful to keep all the reports from the Strangler's previous murders separate from the Coleman murder file. The last thing I wanted was for the media to find out about the Strangler's involvement, at least not yet. When the time was right, I would make the announcement myself. It was always important to keep a firm leash on your case.

When I finished arranging the files to my satisfaction, I took the manila folder with the DNA report, as well as the boxes with the Strangler investigation files, and carried them out of my office and up the stairs into the apartment. In addition to extra clothes and office supplies, I kept a fairly large safe in the apartment's small kitchen. I locked the folder and two of the boxes inside. The remaining two boxes would not fit, so I piled them on top of the safe.

As I walked out of the kitchen, I stopped for a second by the mirror on the wall. I took a fast look. I needed a haircut, but thought my light brown hair looked all right. I ignored the hints of gray on my temples. Obviously, it was just a glare on the cheap mirror.

As I walked back down the steps to the law office, I heard Casey say, "Connor will be with you in just a moment." Then she came walking out of my office toward her desk. She was startled slightly when she saw me, but tried to hide it.

"Who will I be with in a moment?" I asked softly.

"Miss Foster to see you, Mr. Phelan," Casey said in a formal yet sarcastic tone. I took note that Casey was using her maiden name too.

I replied with a grunt that sounded like a mixture of "hmm" and "harumpf," and then walked past her and into my office.

Becky Foster was waiting for me near my desk. She was wearing a navy-blue jumpsuit with small white polka dots that on first glance looked like a dress. It was tight in some areas and loose in others. Her hair hung softly about her shoulders and her smile was as bright as the sun. She was absolutely stunning. When she saw me, she came right over and hugged me firmly.

"Thank you," she said enthusiastically.

"What did I do?" I asked, as we separated. "Not that I'm complaining."

"Well," she said, continuing to smile, "I don't know what you did specifically, but Matt was not around last night at all. It was the first time in weeks."

"Oh. Well, he and I had a discussion last night, and we... well." I paused, looking for the right words. "Let's just say we came to an understanding." I thought I sounded mysterious, though hoped I did not sound cocky.

Becky looked at me carefully, clearing examining both sides of my face. She reached down and took both of my hands. She turned them over and looked at my knuckles.

"What are you looking for?" I asked.

"You don't have cuts on your knuckles or any marks on your face," she answered.

"Why would I?"

"Matt is not exactly an *enlightened* man," Becky said. "He usually punches first and talks later."

"Don't worry about me, Becky," I said, trying to sound confident, "I can take care of myself."

"And of me as well?" she asked.

"When necessary," I replied immediately.

She smiled briefly, but the serious look returned to her face rather quickly. "Please don't get into a fight with him," she pleaded. "He's much bigger than you and I would hate to see you get hurt because of me."

It was nice to hear someone concerned about my well-being. Still, I wasn't sure how much I should tell Becky about my confrontation with Matt Jordan.

Before I could say anything, Becky started talking again. "I've seen Matt in a lot of fights over the years. He's pretty good at it and usually wins—"

"Look," I interrupted, "I told your ex-husband as clearly as I could that he better keep away from you."

Becky laughed almost derisively. "I'm surprised he didn't punch you right then and there."

"He tried," I admitted.

"You blocked it?" she asked.

I nodded.

"What happened next?"

"It doesn't matter," I said, again trying to change the subject. "What matters is that I am pretty sure he will leave you alone."

"And I am very grateful," she said, "but I don't understand how you beat him up. He's so big."

Then her eyes brightened slightly as a thought seemed to form on her face.

"Did you kick him in his bad knee?" she asked. "He hurt his left knee in high school and it never healed right."

I smiled, but did not say anything.

"That's it, isn't it?" she announced rather triumphantly. "You kneecapped him, right?"

"No," I answered with a smile, "You might say I hubcapped him." My pun was really bad, but I thought it was very funny. I refrained from laughing though.

Not being in on the joke, Becky was confused. "You what?"

"Never mind," I announced in a tone signifying a hoped-for end to the conversation. "He was not around last night and that should continue. If he comes back, I want a call right away. Okay?"

"Okay," she said with a big smile, "but what do I owe you for your efforts?"

"Nothing," I said.

She frowned, clearly not happy with my answer. "Can I at least treat you to lunch?" she asked.

"That would be fine, but not today," I said. "I have an appearance in county court shortly and I need to finish getting ready."

"How about tomorrow?" she persisted.

I paused for a moment. Casey had my calendar cleared except for the Coleman murder. I certainly would be busy, but would still need to eat. "All right, lunch tomorrow."

"Then it's a date," Becky said cheerfully.

She asked me to meet her tomorrow at a small café in the center of town. I made a mental note of the time and place, but my thoughts were focused more on her choice of words. A "date" she had said. I was confident she did not mean the word in the traditional or romantic sense, but it bothered me nonetheless.

It was certainly ironic. Back in high school, the idea of going on a date with Becky would have had me walking on clouds.

Now, all these years later, just the casual use of the word in an innocuous way made me decidedly uncomfortable. I tried to assure myself. We were *not* going on a date. It would just be two friends having lunch. That's all. I was not completely convincing myself.

"Connor, are you okay?" Becky asked.

Her question made me realize that I had faded from the conversation and was looking down at the floor. "Huh?" I answered rather stupidly, before catching myself. "Yeah, I'm fine."

"You looked like you were in another world for a second," she said.

"It's this murder case," I lied. "Sometimes it can just overwhelm your thoughts." I cleared my throat before continuing. "I apologize. Won't happen again."

"What murder case?" she asked.

I realized that I had not told her anything about the case, and it was not exactly public knowledge yet that I was the appointed prosecutor. I told Becky about Judge Hardy assigning me the case. I explained how Bob Clancy had been cleared by the DNA test and that I was going to ask the judge to dismiss the murder charge. I carefully and very intentionally left out any mention of the Strangler. There was no sense worrying her and I planned to keep his involvement in the case a secret for as long as I could.

"So, who killed her?" she asked. Becky had always been right to the point. It was one of the things I had liked about her from the moment we first met. Still, I could not tell her just yet.

"I'll find out soon enough," I replied.

My statement was not entirely untrue. Though I knew the Rockfield Strangler was the killer, I had no idea who the Strangler really was. So, what I said was not a lie, though it was kind of splitting hairs. I wondered why I felt so badly only telling Becky this half-truth. I was still considering that when she spoke again.

"How about I go to the courthouse and watch you work?" she asked, catching me very much off guard.

"Why would you want to do that? It's just going to be a hearing in front of the judge. Pretty boring stuff."

"Oh, not at all." Her eyes brightened with excitement. "I love criminal cases. I always watch *Forensic Files* and *NCIS*. When I have time, I love reading books about famous cases."

This was something I never knew about her. "When did you get interested in crime and criminals?"

"Several years ago," she replied. "I went on vacation up at Lake George for a week and I needed something to read. In this small store was a book called *Hauptmann's Ladder* about the Lindbergh kidnapping. I bought it and found it fascinating. Ever since then, I have been hooked on true crime."

Must have been some book, I thought. "Okay," I agreed, "I'm leaving for court in just a few minutes."

She flashed that dazzling smile again.

10

The courtroom was surprisingly busy considering this appearance had been scheduled at nearly the last minute. In addition to the court officers standing by the judge's bench and guarding the door leading to the holding cells, Toupee Ray and a young female attorney I did not know sat at the defense table. Dom Bryce sat across from them at the prosecution table with me. In front of me was just the Brady material folder. I had decided to leave the balance of my file at the office.

Becky was seated directly behind me in the front row of the spectators' gallery. A few rows behind her were several reporters. One I recognized from the local newspaper. A second reporter had a recorder with a microphone emblazoned with the logo of WRFL, Rockfield's only radio station with a local newsroom. I did not know the remaining reporters, though I surmised they were from some of the larger papers in Albany.

Behind the reporters was a man and woman sitting together. The man wore a simple gray suit and the woman a black pair of pants and a plain beige sweater. I recognized them from the press clippings in the file back at my office. They were James and Frances Coleman, the parents of Michelle Coleman.

Before coming over to court, I realized that I had neglected to call them to let them know I would be handling the case. It had been quite rude of me. I should have spoken with them the day I got the assignment.

I called them to introduce myself and explain what was going to happen today. They were both very surprised when I told them that the wrong man had been arrested for their daughter's murder. I did not tell them about the Strangler, but knew I would have to soon.

I advised them that they did not have to be in court today, but they insisted. I promised to meet with them in my office after court. Beyond revealing to them that their daughter's killer was a monster returning after two decades of silence, I very much wanted to interview them. I had read their written statements, but had many questions. It was an absolutely necessary meeting, but I was not looking forward to it.

On the defense side of the gallery sat a number of people. I recognized two women as employees of the public defender's office. The third was a man I had never seen before. He was in his mid-forties and had dark hair parted on the right side. His eyes were a very bright shade of blue. He was dressed in khakis and a dark-blue polo shirt. He sat in the very last row and stared straight ahead at the county seal attached to the far wall. I assumed he was a member of Clancy's family.

The fourth person was none other than J. Robert Worthington himself. Obviously, the district attorney found out about the court appearance and decided to have a look for himself. He sat quietly in a charcoal suit that looked expensive enough to require a bank loan. His gold Rolex glistened from the sunlight coming through the glass windows to his rear left. He glared at me when he noticed I was looking his way. I just smiled politely.

To Worthington's right and left were two young prosecutors

from his office. I had no idea what their names were, but was certain they were there to suck up to their boss.

The sound of clanking metal caught my attention. Robert Clancy was being escorted to the defense table by two sheriff's deputies. He was wearing an orange jail jumpsuit. His ankles were shackled. A thick chain was around his waist and each of his wrists was handcuffed to that chain on either side of his body. He could not move his hands enough to even scratch his belly.

The guards brought him to his chair. Clancy sat and Toupee Ray started talking with his client and the guards. It appeared he was trying to convince the deputies to uncuff one of his client's hands. The taller of the two guards shook his head. Both officers took positions right behind their prisoner, ready to jump into action at the first sign of trouble.

Clancy did not look prepared to offer any resistance. He was unshaven and looked very tired. His eyes were glassy and the only word I could think of to describe him was defeated. He had been in jail many times, but this time it was on a charge of murder. The gravity of his situation was etched on his face.

I was still looking at the defendant when the door to the judge's chambers opened and County Court Judge Hardy walked into the room. Immediately, the court officer standing by the bench shouted, "All rise." As everyone stood and faced the bench, the bailiff continued, "The Linton County Court is now in session. The Hon. John J. Hardy presiding."

Hardy walked behind his bench and sat in the oversized leather chair. He grabbed a large file from the side of his desk and slid it in front of him. He looked down at it through his reading glasses that rested on the very tip of his nose. Then he glanced up and over the spectacles at the still standing audience.

"Oh, be seated, ladies and gentlemen," he said in his boisterous yet friendly voice. When everyone was seated, the judge continued. "For the record, I call the case of the People of the State of New York versus Robert Clancy. The defendant stands charged via indictment for Murder in the First Degree, Burglary in the Second Degree, and two counts of Criminal Possession of Stolen Property in the Fourth Degree. The defendant is present with his attorney, Mr. Stanton. The People are represented by Mr. Phelan."

When Hardy finished with his prolonged announcement, he turned to me. Before he could say another word, Ray Stanton was on his feet.

"Your honor," he protested, "is it really necessary for my client to remain shackled like an animal? I respectfully request that my client's hands be freed so that he may take notes and assist me with his defense."

"I don't think we are going to be here very long, counselor, and we are certainly not taking testimony or presenting evidence today," Hardy responded without even looking at him. "Motion denied."

Stanton resumed his seat and Hardy cleared his throat. "Mr. Phelan?" he croaked. "You asked for this appearance today. Do you have something to offer?"

I stood up. "Yes, your honor," I said in a voice loud enough to be heard throughout the courtroom. "If it please the court, I wish to disclose for the record some important new evidence both to the court and to defense counsel."

I handed one of the copies of the DNA report to Toupee Ray. He started reading the report frantically. The bailiff took the copy for the judge. He moved quickly for an older guy as he brought it right to the bench.

"Your honor," Stanton announced in a voice choked with excitement, "in light of this new evidence, I move—"

"Hold on, counselor," Hardy interrupted. "Allow me to finish reading it first."

"Yes, sir," Ray answered. He remained standing, ready to complete his motion as soon as the judge was ready.

Hardy read the report carefully before closing the folder and placing it on top of his court file. He looked up, ignored the excited defense counsel, and stared directly at me. "Mr. Phelan, is there a reason why you called this hearing today?" Hardy chided, his tone quickly becoming very serious. "You could have disclosed this document via regular mail. I hope you are not wasting the court's time."

I was not sure if he appreciated the importance of the report or if he was just testing me. Often judges will give new attorneys a hard time, almost as a hazing or initiation. I was by no means a beginner, but I had been away from the prosecutor's table for some time. I also had never appeared in court before Hardy as presiding judge. I decided to get right to the point. No sense pussyfooting around.

"Your honor, it was necessary to have the defendant and his attorney present in light of the motion I am about to make."

"Well, out with it," Hardy demanded rather irritably.

The old goat's mood was worsening. I considered, for just a moment, launching into a lengthy statement on criminal justice. I could bust his chops too. But I resisted my temptation.

"Judge, based on this scientific report," I continued, keeping my voice even and without emotion, "the People move to dismiss the murder charge with prejudice."

"What?!" came a shout from the back of the courtroom.

I looked back and DA Worthington was on his feet. His face was bright red and his eyes were wide with anger. "What the hell do you think you're doing?" he screamed at me.

"Mr. Worthington," Hardy bellowed, his face even redder than the district attorney's. "I will not tolerate that kind of behavior in my courtroom. If you ever behave like that again, you will be in contempt of court and will have a seat in my holding cell. Do I make myself clear?"

Worthington remained standing and just stared at the judge. He said nothing.

"Am I clear?" Hardy repeated in an even louder voice.

"Yes," the district attorney finally replied in a tone ripe with resentment and frustration.

"Yes, what?" Hardy demanded.

With his eyes blazing with fury, Worthington answered in a seething voice, "Yes, *sir.*"

The two men continued to glare at one another for a few seconds before Worthington broke eye contact and stormed out of the room.

I was trying very hard not to smile. I had absolutely loved that exchange. Worthington was an elitist snob and needed an occasional trimming of his ego. Being embarrassed and threatened with contempt would do exactly that. I glanced over to the reporters and they were busy writing in their little notebooks. All except one. The reporter from WRFL was scurrying after the district attorney, hoping to get a recorded comment. I hoped he would catch him while he was still burning mad.

"Mr. Phelan?" the judge called out.

I had been enjoying Worthington's embarrassment so much, I had forgotten about Hardy. "Yes, sir," I answered as I turned back to the bench.

"Are you absolutely certain you want to dismiss the murder charge, counselor?" Hardy questioned.

"As a matter of ethics, I have no alternative," I replied. "Bob Clancy did not murder Michelle Coleman."

Hardy just looked at me for a few seconds. Then he picked up his gavel and banged it on his bench. "The charge of murder is hereby dismissed," he announced.

I looked over at Clancy. He was clearly confused, but I could see him beginning to realize what had happened. His eyes filled with tears. Addressing me, he said in a very gravelly voice, "Thank you, sir."

I nodded and looked back to the judge.

"Excuse me, judge," Ray Stanton interjected, "may I be heard, sir?"

"Go ahead, Mr. Stanton," the judge answered.

"Your honor, since my client has been cleared of the charges, I move for his immediate release."

Hardy seemed amused by the request. He turned in his chair and faced me. "Well, counselor, what do you think of them apples?"

I smiled at Hardy's colloquial remark before answering. It was amazing how he could bounce back and forth between being jovial, grumpy, angry, and then jovial again.

"Judge, while Mr. Clancy did not murder Michelle Coleman, he did break into her house and steal her jewelry. The charges of Burglary and Criminal Possession of Stolen Property still stand."

I paused for a second as I considered my next remark. "These are both serious felonies that could result in a long prison term given the defendant's prior felony convictions."

Before I could finish my thought, Ray Stanton interrupted me. "My client is a victim of drugs and alcohol, your honor. Putting him in prison will accomplish nothing."

"Excuse me, counselor," I said in a raised staccato voice, "I wasn't finished yet." I did not like being interrupted by the judge, but I tolerated it because he had the power to put me in jail. I was not about to be interrupted by a mere attorney, however, particularly by one wearing what looked like a muskrat on his head.

"Now," I continued, lowering my voice a bit, "while the charges against Mr. Clancy are still severe, I am willing to consider a plea bargain, which would result in significantly less jail time."

Stanton took in a loud breath to speak, but I cut him right off.

"However, such a deal would be contingent on his successful completion of inpatient drug and alcohol counseling, as well as his cooperation in the prosecution of the real murderer of Michelle Coleman."

"But I don't know nothing about no murder," Clancy's gravelly voice announced. "I broke in and took some shit, but that's it."

Stanton whispered in his client's ear rather forcefully.

"I advise you not to speak, Mr. Clancy," Hardy admonished, "and mind your language. There will be no cussing in my court. You got that?"

"Yes, judge," Clancy answered, his head lowered.

Hardy once again picked up his gavel and banged it loudly. "Deputies, please take the defendant to the holding cell."

As the officers each grabbed one of Clancy's arms, he stood and slowly ambled with them. As he did so, Hardy banged his gavel for the third time. I made a mental note to see if I could sneak back later and break that damn thing.

"I want to see counsel in my chambers," Hardy ordered. "Now."

11

Getting to the judge's chambers was not an easy task. Hardy had his own private exit from the courtroom, but the rest of us had to go out the main door at the far end of the room. All the reporters were waiting there with cameras, recorders, notepads, and tons of questions. It was not an enviable journey.

Before I could even take a step, Toupee Ray came charging over, blocking my way. "Connor, how about he pleads to petit larceny and does six months?" he asked excitedly.

I shook my head and put both hands up, urging him to stop talking. "We'll discuss details of a plea later, Ray," I said. "Right now, let's go see the judge."

He scurried back to his table to collect his briefcase. I asked Dom to give Becky a ride home and then turned toward the flock of reporters. When I got within ten feet of them, they began shouting questions at me.

"What was in that folder you gave the judge?" one reporter shouted. Another screamed out, "Who is the real killer, Mr. Phelan?"

I said "No comment" multiple times before walking out of

the courtroom and into the large outer hallway with the reporters following close behind.

Once again, I found my path blocked. This time it was DA Worthington. His face was still extremely red and it did not look like he had calmed down at all. "What do you think you're doing?" he roared. "Clancy is a guilty man. The case is open and shut."

The reporters immediately went silent, waiting for me to reply. I realized in that moment that whatever I said next was likely going to be in the morning newspaper and might be on the radio news within the hour. Before I could say a word, Worthington was speaking again. His voice was different this time. He too had seen the reporters. Although he was standing directly in front of me, he was speaking to the reporters in a full political campaign-style voice.

"Bob Clancy killed that poor girl in cold blood. I put together an airtight case against him, but due to a legal technicality, my office could not handle the matter any further. Unfortunately, Judge Hardy chose Mr. Phelan to take over the case. It is apparent and obvious that Mr. Phelan lacks the skill and the experience to handle this important matter."

Worthington was addressing the media as if I was not even there. I wanted nothing more than to knock this pompous hypocrite on his ass. I resisted the urge, but felt the temptation growing with each passing second. Finally, realizing that I had to say something, I faced the reporters. "Ladies and gentlemen," I announced, "the evidence in this case proves beyond a shadow of a doubt that Bob Clancy did not kill Michele Coleman."

Worthington laughed derisively and stepped forward so that he was even with me on my left side, though still facing the assembled media. "His fingerprints were at the crime scene and he was caught with the victim's jewelry. He killed her."

I pivoted to the left and got directly in Worthington's face. I spoke my next words slowly and deliberately, using a tone that made it clear that if he interrupted me again, he would do so at his own peril. "Bob Clancy broke into the house and stole jewelry. He remains charged with those crimes. Someone else committed the murder and the evidence I presented to the court today proves that."

To my surprise, the enraged district attorney kept speaking. As he did, I hoped he appreciated the near Herculean effort I was making not to drive my fist through his head. "Your job, young man," Worthington spoke in a condescendingly arrogant tone, "is to convict Clancy, not let him go."

"No," I replied, raising my voice and pointing my finger right at the tip of his nose, "a prosecutor's job is not to just seek convictions. It is a prosecutor's job to seek justice, even if that means an acquittal."

He opened his mouth to speak, said nothing, and closed it again. He appeared to be searching for an answer, but without success.

Before either of us could continue our pleasant discussion, Ethel Bollenbacher's stern voice echoed through the cavernous hallway. "Mr. Phelan, the judge is waiting." She was standing at the door to the judge's chambers with her arms folded across her chest. I was almost surprised she didn't have a ruler in her hand to rap my knuckles.

"Yes, ma'am," I called back politely, and started toward her. As I did, I could hear Worthington resume his conversation with the reporters and continue blasting me. While walking, two thoughts came to my mind. First, what was the mysterious power this schoolmarm had to turn grown men into obedient children? Second, I should have decked that asshole.

I took a seat to the left front of Judge Hardy's desk. Ray Stanton was already seated in the chair to the right.

If Judge Hardy was angry about my tardiness, he neither

showed it nor mentioned it. Instead, he got right to business. "Okay, Mr. Phelan, out with it. If Clancy didn't kill her, who did?"

I paused for a moment. I knew there was a good possibility that Hardy would ask this, but I was hoping to hold back this information a little longer. "I do not have a name for you, judge."

Hardy leaned forward in his chair, put both of his palms flat on his desktop, and lifted himself slightly on his hands. "You dismissed a first-degree murder charge and you don't know who the real murderer is?" he asked angrily. "Is this a joke?"

"No, your honor," I replied, "I know who the murderer is."

"Then who is it?" Hardy demanded, looking slightly confused.

"I don't know his name," I answered, thinking that this conversation was beginning to sound like an Abbott-and-Costello routine.

Judge Hardy was clearly not amused. His already reddened face was darkening. "You just said that you know who the murderer is, did you not?"

"Yes, sir."

"Then tell me his name!" Hardy shouted.

"I don't know his name," I repeated, knowing full well that my answer might cause Hardy's head to blow right off his shoulders. Yet, inside, I was laughing at the almost vaudevillian conversation we were having.

Ray Stanton chose this moment to finally speak. It had been obvious from the moment I sat down that Ray was just dying to talk. Apparently, he could wait no longer. "Judge, can we talk about a possible disposition of my client's case?" he asked.

Hardy spun his chair toward Stanton with surprising speed. "What the hell is the matter with you, you halfwit?" he howled, his temper finally boiling over.

Stanton just stared for a second with his eyes wide with fright. Suddenly, the intercom on the judge's desk buzzed loudly.

Hardy pounded the button and loudly barked, "What do you want?"

"Excuse me, your honor?" Ethel Bollenbacher's annoyed voice asked almost menacingly.

Hardy immediately cleared his throat loudly, trying to regain his composure. "Oh, Miss Bollenbacher," he said apologetically, "pardon me. What can I do for you?"

Even the mighty Judge John J. Hardy is no match for Old Iron Girdle, I thought.

Satisfied with the more contrite tone, Ethel announced, "District Attorney Worthington wishes to see you, judge."

Hardy rolled his eyes and dropped his forehead on the desk with a thud in a gesture of absolute frustration. "Send him in," he groaned.

I will never know how I did not burst out laughing.

Judge Hardy kept his head on his desk and took a few deep breaths. He looked up just as the door opened and Rob Worthington walked in.

"Your honor, I have a matter to discuss with you," he declared.

Hardy put his hands to the sides of his head and slowly massaged his temples. "Just a moment, sir," he said softly and rather slowly, "I'll let you speak in a moment."

Worthington wisely did not argue with the judge. Hardy finished rubbing his head and looked at me directly. "Connor, I want you to tell me who killed Michelle Coleman," he said, "and if you tell me you don't know his name, I will find you in contempt and you will leave here in handcuffs."

I paused for a moment. Now I was stuck. I did not want to announce what Dom and I had discovered, especially in front of that arrogant district attorney. I also had no desire to spend the night in jail. "Okay, judge," I began, "but may I request an instruction to both attorneys present that they may not disclose to anyone what I am about to tell you?"

Hardy nodded, glared at both Worthington and Stanton, and said simply, "So ordered."

I could stall no longer. "Your honor, although I do not know the murderer's name, I can tell you that DNA evidence has proven definitively that the killer is the person known as the Rockfield Strangler."

Hardy actually smiled a little when I finished, while Toupee Ray blurted out, "Holy shit."

Worthington cleared his throat and said, "Well, the case is mine now and I expect you to turn over that evidence to me right away."

"Excuse me," Hardy interjected.

Worthington continued without missing a beat. "Judge, the only reason my office was conflicted out of the case was that my chief assistant previously represented Robert Clancy. While Mr. Phelan is free to take the larceny and burglary charges to trial, the murder investigation once again belongs to my office."

Technically, Worthington was correct. As the elected district attorney, he had authority to prosecute all crimes in Linton County. With Clancy out of the murder case, there was no longer a conflict. Despite that, I was not going to give up my case without a fight.

"Judge, Robert Clancy is still a potential witness in this case," I argued. "He was at the crime scene after the murderer but before the police arrived. His observations and everything he did will be extremely important. Since he is still a part of this case, the district attorney's office is still conflicted out."

"Nonsense," Worthington countered, "a conflict only exists for a defendant, not a witness. I would think Mr. Phelan would know that."

Judge Hardy had now completely regained his composure.

He looked at me and said, "He may have a point, Connor. I only assigned you to prosecute Clancy because of Chief Assistant Alexander's prior representation."

"No," I interrupted loudly. I was not going to let Hardy give my case back to Worthington. I was surprised at how strongly I felt about this. "You did not appoint me to prosecute Bob Clancy," I continued. "You told me you wanted to appoint me to prosecute the murderer of Michelle Coleman and I agreed. I am investigating this murder and plan to see it through to the end."

"Rubbish," Worthington countered, making me once again consider the merits of punching him. "That's just semantics. This case is mine now and you know it."

I felt like I was losing the argument. The idea of Rob Worthington announcing to the world that he was replacing me made me feel sick. I decided to play the only card I had left. "Judge, you know I did not want this case. In fact, I asked you to give it to someone else."

Hardy smiled. "Yes, I remember."

"You asked me to take this case despite my reservations," I said, looking him right in the eyes. "You said you would consider it a personal favor."

"I did indeed, my boy," he replied.

"I agreed as a personal favor to you," I added, putting extra emphasis on the word *personal*, just as Hardy had done that day. "Doesn't that mean something?"

Hardy smiled broadly. "You bet it does, Connor, and I shall return that very favor. The case remains yours."

Worthington's eyes went wide in disbelief. "This is outrageous!" he shouted. "You can't do this!"

"But I can," Hardy retorted, "and I just did."

The two men once again locked eyes for a moment before Worthington grunted and stormed out of the room, closing the door loudly behind him.

Hardy chuckled and then turned back to me. "Funny how hard you fought to keep a case you insisted you never wanted," he said. "Guess you're getting some of that fire back."

I said nothing, but the comment hit home. I had argued strongly against getting this assignment. Now I was fighting just as hard to keep the case. What had changed?

I was still pondering this when Toupee Ray broke the silence. "So, can we talk about a plea bargain now?"

I thought, *What the hell is the matter with you, you halfwit?* Hardy must have been thinking the same thing because he broke into a broad smile.

12

I spent another twenty minutes or so in the judge's chamber working out an agreement. It was finally decided that Clancy would be sent to inpatient rehabilitation at St. Maximilian Kolbe Hospital, a well-respected facility up near the Canadian border. He would agree to tell us anything and everything he saw on the night of the murder. If he successfully did both, he would be allowed to plea to one count of burglary in the third degree. He would still have to go to state prison as his prior felony record mandated it, but would receive only a minimal sentence.

Clancy would remain in the county jail for forty-eight hours before his transfer, so that Dom Bryce could thoroughly interview him and lock down his story.

When the details of the deal were in place, the judge scheduled the next court appearance and sent us on our way. Stanton went to speak to his client in the holding cell. I had little doubt that Ray would make sure his client took the offer. If he refused, I could convict him of burglary and possession of stolen property with little difficulty. Since he had two prior felonies on his record, he could face the three-strikes-and-you're-out rule. That could mean twenty-five years to life. Bob Clancy was not the sharpest knife in the drawer, but he had been around long enough to know that a maximum of three years was a better bet than risking a life sentence. He would take the deal.

I was getting ready to follow Stanton out the door when Judge Hardy asked me to stick around. He ordered me to close the door and have a seat. I did so.

Hardy stared at me for a few minutes before he finally spoke. "I was wondering how long it would take you to figure out that the Rockfield Strangler was back," he said with a wry smile.

I was stunned. *He already knew?* "How did you know?" I asked.

"Don't forget, Connor," the judge replied, "I was the district attorney when that son of a bitch started killing. It was before you came to my office, but I still remember it. As soon as I heard from Bills about the placement of the hunting knife, I knew it was him."

"Bills told you?" I stammered. "But he works for Worthington."

Hardy got a very satisfied look on his face before continuing. "Connor, my boy," he said, "Roger Billingsley worked for me for many years. I wanted to have him as one of my court officers, but he refused. He likes catching the bad guys and is not yet ready to give it up. So when he saw this file, he came to my home to let me know his thoughts about it. He felt that Worthington was too caught up with the fingerprint evidence and was unable to see the big picture through his desire for a fast conviction—"

"Wait a minute," I interrupted, "Bills knew it was the Rockfield Strangler?"

"No, no," Hardy corrected, "Bills never worked on that case. That was Dom Bryce's case. Bills just didn't believe Clancy was a murderer. His greatest strength has always been his ability to read people. That's why I always had him with me whenever I picked a jury. He didn't think Clancy did it, so I asked him to give me all the details. Once he mentioned the hunting knife, I just knew it."

"That was Dom's reaction as well," I offered.

Hardy pointed both of his hands toward me palm up and gave me a look that suggested I had just hit the target. And suddenly, I understood. "That's why you appointed me to this case, isn't it?" I asked accusingly. "You knew I would have Dom as my investigator and he would come to the same conclusion that you did."

"Well, that's partially correct," Hardy answered with a smile. "I also knew you would figure it out as well. The other reason was that you needed it. You were ready to move on with your life and career. You just needed a good swift kick in the ass."

I didn't reply because I knew he was a hundred percent correct. Melissa died over ten years ago. I thought about her frequently, but my memories were more of the happy times than her death. Working as a prosecutor wasn't going to change anything. But intentionally avoiding county court was serving only to focus myself on her death. Melissa would have wanted me to live my life and move on.

I was still considering all of this when Hardy broke the silence. "So, now you know why I assigned you this case."

"You could have just told Worthington and let him catch the guy," I offered.

"Worthington?" Hardy answered, breaking into hearty laughter. "He couldn't find his own ass with two hands and a flashlight."

We both laughed for a few seconds before Hardy said, "All right, my boy, get out there and catch that killer."

I walked to the door, but stopped just as I opened it. The judge was examining some papers on his desk. "John," I said softly to get his attention. He looked up at me, surprised I had again called him by his first name. I smiled, and choking up slightly said, "Thanks."

Hardy gave his jovial smile and answered, "Anytime, my boy, anytime."

I closed the door behind me, nodded to Miss Bollenbacher, and stepped out into the hall expecting to meet a barrage of reporters. To my relief, they had left. So had Worthington. I went down the steps and out the front door. Now out of the courthouse, I thought for a moment about the events that had just taken place.

Just days ago, I was furious at John J. Hardy for assigning me this case. Now I was grateful he had done so. I was again feeling a fire I had thought long since burned out. I was going to solve this mystery and unmask the Rockfield Strangler. I smiled thinking about it.

I paused for only a moment. I still had to meet with Michelle Coleman's parents and it was unlikely either of them would be smiling. So, I turned right and started walking toward my office.

The man in the khakis and dark-blue polo shirt sat in his car watching when Connor Phelan left the courthouse. He had been waiting for him ever since the officer locked up the courtroom. After all the attorneys went to speak to the judge, he had waited patiently to see if the hearing would resume. When it was clear it would not, he had gone to his car to wait.

The dismissal of the murder charge against that drunken old fool Clancy had been an unwelcome development. He had waited so terribly long to kill again. For years, he had been forced to deal with his rage by killing animals; stray cats and dogs mostly. Once in a while, he caught a chicken or a wild turkey. When he choked the animals and their necks broke, it gave him some relief. It allowed just a bit of his pain and anguish to be released.

It was not the same as killing a woman, though. The struggle, the eventual loss of consciousness as he choked her, and the final breath before death was his ultimate release. It would not end his pain or rage, but it would weaken it. He would be able to function for a few months before it grew in intensity and had to be sated again.

Killing a dog or a cat only offered a week or two of release. Yet, it was what he had been forced to do ever since that Allen girl had survived. She was the one woman he seemed unable to kill. She lived through their first encounter only by sheer chance when those two punks interrupted him. If it had been just one, he could have handled him, but not two. So, he had fled, his anger unreleased and growing.

The next evening, he saw a report on the nightly news. The Allen girl had given a description and there on the television was a sketch drawn by the police. He remembered the fear tingling through his arms when he saw his own face in that sketch. She could identify him. She could lead the police to him. If they caught him, he would spend the rest of his life in jail. He would be unable to kill anyone or anything and the anger and rage within him would grow until it consumed him. It would burn him completely out of this existence and torture him throughout all eternity. He could not allow it. He would find Amy Allen and kill her.

He had tried. He remembered how hard he had tried. For weeks he stalked her, looking for the right opportunity. Finally, almost a month after his failure to kill her, he saw his chance. He was driving past her house and there she was. She was sitting on her front porch, completely alone.

He drove further down the street and parked. He got his hunting knife out of the glove compartment and started walking toward her house. The closer he got to her, the more his excitement and rage grew. He was going to get his release. He would be saved from his anger, madness, and despair for a while longer.

He was only a few hundred feet away when a police car drove up and stopped in front of the girl's house. He froze. Had this been a trap? He watched in utter helplessness as that wretched girl came down off her porch and walked to the passenger window of the cruiser. As she leaned in to speak with the officer, it became clear to her would-be killer that he could not kill her. It was as if she was cursed.

He immediately went back to his car and drove home. He parked in the driveway and just sat in the car as he felt the anguish burning from within like white-hot fire. He had brought it all to the surface in preparation for the kill, but had been unable to release it. Now he suffered as his own memories flooded over him like waves of searing pain.

He saw himself driving his family car with his wife sitting next to him and his daughter in the back sitting in her child's seat. He once again saw the tractor trailer lose control in the oncoming lane and lurch toward him. For what seemed like the millionth time, he felt the impact as the huge truck hit the front of the passenger side of his car, lifted up, and ran over it like it was just a large speed bump. In his memory, he could hear the sickening sounds of his wife and daughter being crushed under tons of metal, glass, and plastic. He recalled being stuck inside the crushed vehicle, unable to move. The only thing he could see, other than the debris from his ruined car, was his wife's face covered in blood with her lifeless eyes staring out into nothingness.

He screamed as he relived his nightmare. Tears poured down his cheeks as he pleaded with his own mind to stop showing him these horrible things. He knew he could only stop the pain by killing.

That was the night that he killed his first animal, a stray dog. He lured it into his home with a piece of raw meat. Once it had been fed and fallen asleep in his kitchen, he came up behind it and choked it. The bones in its throat were crushed before it could even offer a defense. He did not bother using his hunting knife after the dog was dead. That ritual was only for young women. The dog was unworthy.

He too was unworthy. Once he had been successful. He had been Charles Edward Duncan, a bank teller and a future vice-president of the Rockfield Bank. Now he was reduced to slaughtering animals to stem the excruciating pain from the memories of the car accident that killed his wife and daughter, and left him impotent, unable to ever have a family again.

For over fifteen years, he lived this way. He killed any animals he could get his hands on. The only way to offer genuine relief was to kill a woman. Yet, he somehow knew deep in his very being that he could never kill another woman, as long as Amy Allen lived. She was a talisman against him. If he killed a woman, he would be caught and spend eternity in a jail cell suffering unimaginable pain.

Then in February 2015, he was reading the local newspaper and saw that Amy Allen had died. The article said it was a drug overdose. He felt elation and concern at the same time. The talisman was gone. Yet, in his mind, he felt it might be a trap. He would wait and bide his time before doing what he knew he must do.

It was over three years later until he felt safe to try again. Even then, he took many months selecting his victim. He finally chose her at a Rockfield High School football game. Michelle Coleman, the pretty blonde cheerleader, caught his eye. He followed her home after the game to determine where she lived. He watched her house for two weeks until he saw his chance. The girl's parents were out and the pretty young thing was alone at home.

He remembered the moment he grabbed her around her neck and squeezed. It was a release like he had never experienced before. Her last breath had sent shivers down his spine and he kept squeezing her neck for minutes after she was already dead. His hands trembled while he stripped her. He gazed at her beautiful body for a long time before pulling out his knife. He plunged it into her just above her vulva into her uterus to tell the world that this girl would never bear his children or anyone else's children.

He watched the television news, listened to the radio, and read all the local newspapers. He was desperate to find out if the talisman of Amy Allen would lead to his capture or if she was truly gone and he was free to resume his killing.

A few days later, the local television news reporter announced that, after the upcoming commercial, they would discuss a major development in the Michelle Coleman murder. The commercials seemed to take forever and he felt himself sweat profusely. Were they looking for him? Was the Allen talisman still alive?

He recalled the feeling of elation when the news broadcast resumed and announced the arrest of Bob Clancy for the murder and played the quote from DA Worthington saying the matter was open and shut. It was really true. The curse of Amy Allen had ended with her death. Bob Clancy would go to prison. Feeling once again able to consider himself as Charles Edward Duncan, as opposed to a nameless animal killer, he was now free to kill again should his pain grow to the point of needing release.

Today's events had potentially ruined all of it. He had heard on his police scanners that the county deputies were bringing

Clancy to the courthouse for an appearance. He assumed this meant a plea deal, so he hurried to the courtroom to see this for himself. Once Clancy was put away, there would be no more investigation and he could make himself ready for the next time his need surfaced.

His first surprise was learning that Connor Phelan was handling the case and not the man on the news who proclaimed the matter "open and shut." Though initially concerned, he assumed that such a simple matter had been referred to an assistant district attorney.

When he heard Phelan announce new evidence and seek dismissal of the murder charge, Duncan was stunned. How could this be happening? Before he could react further, he heard the angry outburst from the district attorney and understood that this other man, this Connor Phelan, had somehow taken control of the case and was ruining everything. He could not allow this to happen. He had waited too long. He would not be reduced to a nameless hunter of cats and dogs.

Later, as he sat in his car waiting for his new nemesis to come out, he thought about the earlier proceedings. What was in that folder given to the judge that caused the dismissal? He had listened to the argument outside the courtroom between Phelan and Worthington. They had come close to discussing this mystery evidence, but had never given any real detail.

He was still pondering this riddle when he saw Connor Phelan descending the courthouse steps. He watched closely as Phelan stopped on the sidewalk, smiled, and then turned down the street away from Duncan's car.

What was he smiling about, Duncan wondered. Did he know who really killed the blonde cheerleader or did he just know it was not the old drunk? Duncan did not know, but would keep an eye on Phelan to find out.

Duncan felt the pain within him beginning to build. He

knew from experience that he had only a week or two before it became unbearable and would have to be set free. He would select the woman soon. He would not go back to killing animals and he would not allow himself to be caught. Amy Allen was dead, and he would not allow Connor Phelan to become a new talisman against him. He would kill him first.

13

I spent the rest of the afternoon meeting with James and Frances Coleman. I let them in on the involvement of the Strangler, but made them promise not to reveal anything to the public. I also promised them I would bring their daughter's killer to justice. As they left my office, I hoped that I could deliver on that promise.

I was just about to leave for the day when Casey walked into my office. I could tell by the look in her eyes that something was wrong. "What is it?" I asked.

"It's that damn Judge Marino," she answered angrily. "He's being a real pain in the ass."

Judge Marcus Marino was a city court judge with delusions of grandeur. He was also well known for having a tragic and chronic case of black robe disease. Black robe disease is a slang term that describes how some attorneys become arrogant and condescending assholes on receiving their black judge's robes. Marino, on the very first day he wore the robe, fined his former law partner $500 for being two minutes late for court. He loved to scream and yell at young attorneys just to make them squirm.

"Well, that's no big shocker," I said, "but what has he done now?"

Casey scowled and replied, "He changed his mind about postponing the Matias trial."

Jose Matias was a client who had been assigned to me a few months ago. He was a low-level dealer of crack cocaine who had been to prison multiple times. He was arrested for selling what appeared to be two pieces of crack cocaine to an undercover state trooper.

Fortunately for Matias, when his product was tested, it was negative for cocaine or any other controlled substance. Matias was apparently desperate for money and mixed some soap and baking soda. He then wrapped the mixture to look like small pieces of crack cocaine.

The case was referred to City Court, where my client was charged with violating section 3383 of the New York Public Health Law. That provision of law makes it a Class A misdemeanor to manufacture, sell, or possess with the intent to sell, an imitation controlled substance. He had been held on bail for three months. If convicted, the most he could get was a year and he would get out after nine months. The only offer made was for six months, which would have him out in four. He had steadfastly refused all offers.

"What time is the case set for?" I asked.

"9am sharp on Monday morning," Casey responded, "and Marino's clerk said the judge plans to take the bench at exactly that time."

Typical Judge Marino, I thought. My original plan was to meet Dom Bryce at the jail and sit in on his questioning of Bob Clancy. So much for that.

"Okay, Casey, it's no big deal—"

"No big deal?" Casey interrupted loudly. "It's on for trial. That douchebag agreed to move the trial and now he changes his mind at the last minute. You haven't even had time to prepare."

I put my hand up to cut her off. "No problem," I said. "I appreciate your concern, but I can handle the case. Just get me the file and I'll look at it tonight or over the weekend at home."

Casey left to get the file, muttering as she left about Judge Marino and what he could do with his attitude. Some of the word combinations she used would have made the cussing hall of fame. It was quite impressive, and I laughed in spite of myself.

Once I had the Matias file, I got in my Cherokee and drove to The Cardinal for dinner. Though I would have to spend my evening reading about fake crack cocaine, I was not going to miss my planned meal. I had already eaten my last frozen dinner and what food I had left was old enough now to grow legs of its own.

I parked in the lot behind The Cardinal and went in through the back door. Eddie Astorino was in his usual spot behind the bar. "Hey Clubber," he yelled, before breaking into the theme from *Rocky*.

"What's that all about?" I asked.

Eddie broke into a big grin. "You know fucking well what it's about. You kicked Matt Jordan's big fat ass the other night."

When I did not initially respond, Eddie pointed to the nearest barstool and said, "Come on, brother, sit down right here and give me a blow-by-blow account."

"How do you even know about it anyway?" I asked as I sat down.

"I run a bar," Eddie replied. "Don't you think I hear things?"

I just glared at him and he got the message very quickly.

"Okay, okay," he continued, "two of the guys from the garage where Matt works stopped in. They said you went all Bruce Lee on him and really fucked up the garage too."

I really did not want to talk about it, but I knew Eddie would never let it go. "All right, boss, bring my dinner and I'll tell you about it while I eat."

Within ten minutes, Eddie served me his usual special— linguini with red clam sauce, and an ice-cold beer to wash it down. Though I still was not thrilled to talk about the fight, I felt better doing so because Eddie's red clam sauce was the best around. Eddie never put extra clams still in the shells into the dish. I always hated that. Plus, he used a combination of spices taught to him by his mother that gave the sauce its signature kick.

After I had three or four bites, I started telling Eddie about my encounter with the big former football player. He listened attentively, though nearly fell to the floor laughing when I described Matt slamming into the hubcap display.

When I finished the story, he grabbed my left hand, held it up, and yelled out, "The champion of the world, Connor 'Clubber' Phelan!" He made sounds like a roaring crowd.

I pulled my hand away. "Will you cut that out?"

"Aw, don't be modest, Clubber," he continued, "you kicked his ass."

I didn't respond, but inside I felt pretty good. I had kicked that jerk's ass. I had always wanted to, but never had the chance. I knew part of it was envy because Becky had married him without ever knowing about my high school crush. To be fair, I never told her.

On the other hand, notwithstanding my own personal petty jealously, Matt had it coming. He had slapped Becky around and made her life miserable. As I thought about it, I felt my hands curling into fists.

"Listen," Eddie said, bringing me out of my thoughts, "watch your ass. Those two guys said that Jordan has not stopped talking about how badly he plans to hurt you. I know you can take care of yourself, but he is one big motherfucker."

I smiled. "Thanks for the tip, boss," I said. "I'll keep an eye open."

We continued talking for the next thirty or forty minutes while I finished my dinner. As always, it was delicious. I nursed the one beer through the meal and rejected two or three suggestions of a refill. I had to read a file tonight and did not want my thoughts clouded by beer. Eddie had fresh cannoli for dessert. It was a simply wonderful meal.

I left Eddie's bar and drove home. As I came up Mountainview Lane, I saw a familiar rusted-out Ford F-150 pickup parked in front of my house. Matt Jordan was standing by his driver's door waiting for me. *Boy, Eddie wasn't kidding,* I thought, as I parked my Cherokee right behind the truck.

Jordan started walking toward me even before I had finished parking. I did not want to be stuck in the car while he threw punches, so I threw open my door and got out quickly. I wasn't quite fast enough. He threw an overhand right and I knew I wasn't going to be able to block it. I turned hard to my left, ducked my head and shrugged my shoulders in an attempt to dodge it. It struck me partially on my right ear and shoulder. It knocked me sprawling, but I was able to roll and come up on my feet. My ear was buzzing and I could feel blood trickling down my neck.

Jordan kept coming at me. I backed away to give myself some space. I took a strong stance, ready to defend. Without warning, I felt something hit me from behind across my head, neck, and shoulders. I was knocked forward and Jordan took the opportunity to punch me square in my left eye. I fell to the ground and could already feel my eye swelling.

Matt had apparently decided not to face me one-on-one. Instead, he had someone hiding who waited until my back was turned to strike. I was very stunned from the punch and was trying to get my bearings when Jordan yelled out, "Get that piece of shit up!"

A pair of strong arms grabbed me and started pulling me up. As soon as I was on my feet, the second guy pulled my arms behind me so Matt would have a wide-open target. Jordan walked confidently toward me. He grabbed my chin with his left hand and lifted me up so I was looking into his eyes. With his right hand, he reached into his back pocket and pulled out a knife.

"Now, you scumbag," he growled. "I am going to cut up that pretty face."

He let go of my face and used his left hand to snap open the blade. It wasn't very big, but it was more than enough to cut me to ribbons.

As he came at me with the knife, I could hear Becky Foster's voice in my head from our conversation in my office the other day. *Did you kick him in his bad knee? He hurt his left knee in high school and it never healed right.*

Matt grabbed my face again with his left hand and brought the knife up with his right. As he did, I threw a right front kick as hard as I could that struck him in the center of his left knee, causing his leg to straighten and his knee to hyperextend. He screamed, dropped the knife, and fell to the ground, holding his knee.

My sudden movement had caused my other attacker to lose his grip. I reached back, grabbed as much of his right shoulder as I could. I pulled him forward and dropped to my right knee as I did. He came right over my shoulder and crashed to the concrete right next to Jordan. I struck him right between the eyes with a knife hand chop. He went still.

I got to my feet. I was still very woozy and my eye must have been swollen shut because I could see almost nothing out of it.

The right side of my face and neck was now covered in blood. I was having trouble standing.

Matt Jordan had also gotten to his feet, though he was having trouble putting weight on his left leg. He had also retrieved the knife. He hobbled toward me, unwilling to give up.

"Matt," I said, "it's over."

"Fuck you," he growled, and slashed at my face with the knife.

I blocked his attack with two hands. I pulled him forward with my right hand and wrapped my left arm over his elbow. As he came forward, he lost his balance. I pinned his elbow under my left armpit and lightly pulled his hand against me. This caused his elbow to slightly hyperextend. He grunted.

"Drop the knife," I ordered, "drop it or I will break your arm."

Instead of dropping it, he tried to hit me with his left fist. "Fuck you!" he yelled again. Obviously, he had a limited vocabulary. Since he would not drop the knife, I had to do it for him. I pulled his hand again, but this time much harder. He screamed as the tendons in his elbow gave way with a loud pop, and he dropped the knife.

I kicked the knife away from him and pushed him flat on the ground. I staggered back and checked on his companion. He was still unconscious. I got my cell phone out and called 911. Matt Jordan and his friend would have to go to the hospital. Frankly, so would I.

The operator answered and I gave my name and address, and requested the police and two ambulances. No sooner had I disconnected the call when Matt got to his feet. His right arm hung dead at his side. He was limping badly on his left leg. Yet, he was still coming after me. I could not believe it.

When he finally came within a few feet of me, I said, "Just stay down, Matt."

He gave the same response as before and threw a wild left haymaker at me. It was clumsy and awkward. He put all of his weight into the punch and his entire body lunged forward. I ducked the punch and slipped behind him. I grabbed him around the neck, pulled him back, and applied a basic chokehold. He struggled for a few seconds before losing consciousness. I eased him down to the concrete and let him go. He lay motionless.

I backed away from both men and sat down on the other side of the road. I was getting dizzy, either from loss of blood or from a concussion from Matt's punch. Whatever it was, I had to sit down. I waited for the ambulances and the police, hoping that Matt Jordan would stay down this time. He did.

A minute or two later, I saw flashing red lights approaching. It was the last thing I saw before everything went black.

Charles Edward Duncan sat quietly a few hundred yards from the remains of the fight. He had followed Phelan since picking him up at the courthouse. He needed to learn all he could about this man before he became a new talisman.

He had followed his nemesis to Mountainview Lane. When Connor drove in behind the old truck, Duncan had pulled his car over and parked. He was close enough to watch, but far enough to avoid drawing attention to himself.

He had seen the two men attack. They were both big men and he had hoped they would destroy Phelan for him. He had smiled broadly when the bigger of the two men pulled out his knife.

He watched in amazement as Phelan fought back and defeated both men. It was not until he saw Connor lock in his chokehold that he became truly frightened. This was the same choke he used on his victims. Once applied, there was no escape.

There could be no doubt. Connor Phelan was sending him a message. He was the talisman, the one who could stop him forever. Duncan felt his pain grow a little more as he thought. He did not have much more time, but knew he could not kill his enemy on his own. Phelan had just defeated two men far bigger than Duncan.

He needed to find a weakness, a vulnerability. Once he found it, he would bring Connor Phelan to his end. He would hear his final breath as he choked the life out of him. Then he would have his release. Maybe this was the death that would end his pain forever.

14

I woke at the Rockfield Medical Center. The clock on the wall read 7am and I realized I had been brought by ambulance the night before. I had vague recollections of receiving stitches on my right ear. The sucker punch from behind had ripped it open.

As I sat up, my head hurt so badly I felt nauseous. I still could barely see out of my left eye. My right hand had a bandage on it too. I must have cut it during the struggle, though I could not remember doing so.

To my right, I saw a man sitting on a chair lightly dozing. It was Dom Bryce.

"Hey, sleepyhead," I croaked.

Dom jerked awake. He smiled when he saw I was up. "Boy, do you look like shit, pal," he offered cheerily.

I laughed a little, though it hurt terribly to do so. "You should see the other guys," I said.

"Well, the one guy is not too bad," Dom replied. "You just broke his nose. But Jordan is all kinds of fucked up."

"My heart bleeds," I said. "The son of a bitch pulled a knife and was going to cut off my nose and shove it up my ass."

Dom laughed loudly and it rang through my head like a

gong. "Jordan paid the price, pal," he continued. "His knee has got two ligament tears, and his elbow is broken. He's in surgery right now, and when he gets out, he's going to be arrested for attacking you with a knife."

"It's just my word against him and his friend though," I offered.

"No way," Dom interrupted, "I had a little conversation with his buddy, a guy named Toman. He cried like a baby right after I told him how guys like him get bent over and fucked in prison. He gave Jordan up and told the whole story."

I smiled. *Well, at least I don't have to worry about him,* I thought.

A nurse brought me a breakfast of eggs, bacon, toast, and coffee. It was by no means gourmet, but I was hungry enough not to care.

As I started to eat, Dom got up to leave. "I have to get over to the county jail, pal. I have to interview that mutt, Clancy. He's being shipped off to prison tomorrow, and I have to see if he knows anything."

That seemed odd. I thought Dom was seeing him on Monday. *Must have been moved up,* I thought.

"Get as much detail as you can," I advised, "maybe we can—"

Dom held up his hand to signal me to stop talking. "Not my first rodeo, Connor. You just do something about your face," he said with a smirk as he walked out the door.

I consider yelling something to him, but my headache convinced me that yelling was not a good idea. So, I went back to my meal.

I was just finishing my coffee when Casey Franklin and Becky Foster came walking in. Casey was carrying a garment bag and a pair of my shoes. I recognized the bag as my emergency suit. I always kept a clean set of clothes for court in the apartment above my office.

Becky saw my face and stopped in her tracks. Her brown eyes filled with tears. Her lips trembled as she tried to speak, but nothing came out.

"No reason to cry, Becky," I said, "I'm not that ugly."

She laughed just a little, though it was mixed with tears. "This is my fault," she cried.

I cut her right off. "Absolutely not," I said, raising my voice. "This is all about Matt Jordan. He and one of his buddies came after me. I took care of both of them. Matt will probably be going to prison, so my business with him is finished."

She sat next to me on the bed. She leaned in and kissed me on the cheek. "Thank you," she whispered.

I was thinking of what to say when Casey's voice echoed through my head. "Connor, you need to get up and get dressed, right now," she said urgently. "You have to be in court in less than an hour."

"What are you talking about?" I asked in surprise. "It's Saturday morning."

"Saturday?" Casey asked in surprise. "Didn't Mr. Wonderful tell you? Figures he would leave it to me."

I stared at her for a moment in confusion. "Tell me what?" I asked. "What the hell is going on?"

"You've been in the hospital and in and out of consciousness for the last two days," Casey replied. "It's Monday morning."

I was stunned. "Monday?"

Becky took my hand. "You were diagnosed with a bad concussion," she said. "You were hit with a metal bar."

I looked at Casey. She nodded. "One of those scumbags hit you with it. The police found it at the scene covered in your blood."

I was still trying to wrap my head around the fact that I had lost two days when Casey took my other arm. "Come on, Connor, you have to get to court. The Matias case, remember?"

I shook my head and said, "I just woke up after two days and am expected in court? Just tell Judge Marino what happened."

"I already did," Casey answered immediately. "That prick fuck said he doesn't care. He says the trial is happening this morning with or without you."

"I don't even have my file. How am I supposed to—"

"I have it," Casey responded. "I grabbed it from your car this morning. Now get ready."

"Yes, ma'am," I said, grabbing my garment bag and shoes, and heading for the bathroom. It took me quite some time to get dressed because I was still very woozy. When I was finished, I took a look at myself in the mirror. My left eye was swollen and purple. There were several stitches above my eye. When I turned my head to the left, I could see the stitches in my right ear. Even in my pinstriped navy suit and sharp red tie, I was far from handsome.

As I walked out of the bathroom, my head throbbed. I made a mental note to file a complaint against Judge Marino for this.

When I was leaving, my assigned nurse objected. She felt strongly that I should remain in the hospital until cleared by a doctor. I told her I completely understood, but had no choice under the circumstances. I signed myself out against doctor's orders (really just my nurse), and Casey and Becky helped me to the elevator and then into Casey's car. Becky went to her own car to follow us.

I read quickly through the case folder while Casey drove like a maniac through the streets of Rockfield. I was really angry at being forced to do this trial. I was not sure how I would handle it without proper preparation, but when I saw the prosecutor's witness list, I was confident I had nothing to worry about.

We arrived at city court and walked through the front doors

with less than a minute to spare. My client was sitting at the defense table attired in his orange jail jumpsuit with chains and shackles holding him in place.

When I said hello, he just stared at me wide-eyed. "What the fuck happened to you, man?" he asked, in a thick Mexican accent.

"Trial prep," I answered quickly before taking my seat.

I had only just barely sat down when the judge's door flew open and Judge Marino strode into the courtroom. I stood back up as the bailiff called the session to order. Marino called the case and then glared at me. "Mr. Phelan, is the defense ready to proceed?"

"Yes, judge," I answered, unwilling to call this jerk *your honor*.

After the prosecutor, a young kid just out of law school named Jenkins, asserted his readiness for trial, Judge Marino said, "I guess we can bring in the potential jurors now."

"That will not be necessary, judge," I asserted. "My client waives trial by jury."

Marino looked surprised. He looked at my client. "Do you want me or a jury to decide your guilt, Mr. Matias?"

Matias looked at me and I nodded slightly in affirmation. Then he answered the judge saying, "I agree with my lawyer, sir."

"Very well," the judge thundered, "Mr. Jenkins, call your first witness."

The first witness was a female state trooper. She testified how she had arranged to buy crack cocaine from my client. She had given him two twenty-dollar bills with the serial numbers recorded. She even testified to the serial numbers from memory. She was an impressive witness.

She identified the two white lumps wrapped in plastic that she said came from Matias. They were entered into evidence when I declined to object.

When Jenkins finished his direct examination, the judge turned to me. "Cross examination?"

I stood and walked to the podium between the two tables. I leaned slightly into the microphone and said, "No questions, judge."

Marino looked at me almost suspiciously before saying, "Very well. Call your next witness, Mr. Jenkins."

As I slowly walked back to my table, I looked quickly out into the audience behind me. Becky and Casey were both sitting in the second row. I smiled and winked at them before sitting down. I was trying to let them know I was fine when in reality I felt like I might fall to the floor.

The second witness was another state trooper who was equally impressive. He was the arresting officer. He described in exquisite detail how he had observed what he thought was a drug sale, and then took my client into custody. He also said he recovered the buy money from the suspect's right front pocket. This left little doubt that Matias had been the one who made the sale.

When Jenkins finished, I again walked to the podium and announced I had no questions. Judge Marino scowled at me as I returned to my chair. When I got there, Matias leaned over to speak to me. "What are you doing, man? Ain't you gonna ask no questions?"

I put my hand on his shoulder and smiled. "Relax, Jose," I said reassuringly, "just trust me. You are going home today."

He said nothing, but just leaned back in his chair.

The third witness was yet another state trooper. He had used a digital recorder to film the entire transaction. After only a few questions, the prosecutor asked to play the video. He had not set a sufficient legal foundation, so the judge looked to me for an objection.

I stood and said, "It's okay, judge. I have no objection. He can play the tape."

Marino looked like he wanted to jump over the bench and strangle me. But he ordered the bailiff to play the tape. Sure enough, it showed exactly what both of the first two witnesses described. There was Jose making a sale to the undercover officer.

When the tape ended, Jenkins announced that he was finished with his witness. The judge looked over to me. "I don't suppose you have any questions for this witness?" he asked sarcastically.

I stood, put on my most patronizing smile, and said, "Actually, I don't. Thank you." As I sat down, Matias looked at me, almost pleading with me to do something. I mouthed the word *relax* to him.

Mr. Jenkins seemed very surprised. So far, he had called three witnesses. I had neither objected nor asked a single question of them. In fact, I had done absolutely nothing. When the judge asked for his next witness, Jenkins almost meekly said, "Well, judge, I guess the prosecution rests."

This time, instead of simply looking at me, Judge Marino turned his chair toward me. He leaned forward on his bench and said, "Do you plan to even call a witness, Mr. Phelan?"

I stood up and very slowly walked to the microphone at the podium. I deliberately took my time, knowing full well that it was making the judge crazy. When I finally got to the podium, I tapped the microphone lightly just to make sure it was on. I got exactly the effect I wanted. The annoying sound of feedback echoed through the court.

"Oh, sorry, judge," I said.

"Mr. Phelan," the judge demanded, "are you going to call any witnesses or not?"

"No, judge," I replied, "but I would like to make a motion at this time."

"Go ahead," Marino answered.

"I move to dismiss the charges against my client as the prosecution has failed to make out a prima facie case. I would ask the court to examine my client's rap sheet, which I am sure is in the court's file."

"The court is well aware of your client's record, Mr. Phelan," Marino responded with annoyance, "but I am not sure what relevance that—"

"Well, judge," I interrupted, causing him to glare at me yet again, "that record shows that my client has been convicted repeatedly for selling drugs. My client's apparent chosen profession is dealing drugs."

I glanced over at Jose and he looked decidedly uncomfortable. I didn't feel too badly for him. He was going to be getting out of jail in just a few hours. I addressed the judge. "My client is honest in his work. He never sells shoddy merchandise," I continued, taking time to point at the plastic evidence bags. "I respectfully submit, judge, that the white substances in those baggies are in fact crack cocaine."

Jose jumped to his feet. "Wait a minute. Wait a minute!" he cried out. "You are trying to send me to prison. You are making up a story."

The two guards behind him grabbed him by the shoulders and pulled him back into his seat.

"Keep your client under control, Mr. Phelan!" Marino shouted.

I was not having any of it. Even though it caused my head to almost explode, I shouted right back. "He is just upset because his honesty as a drug dealer has been questioned!"

Marino was less than pleased at my interruption or my shouting. "What are you talking about, counselor?" he roared.

"What I am talking about is Criminal Law 101!" I shouted back. "The prosecutor must prove every element of the charges beyond a reasonable doubt. My client is charged with possessing an imitation controlled substance. Well, I say that that is cocaine. It is the real McCoy."

Now the prosecutor was on his feet. "Your honor," he protested, "that substance was tested for cocaine and came back negative."

"Objection, judge," I countered. "Assumes facts not in evidence. We have not heard from a lab technician. There is no scientific report in evidence. I say the substance is cocaine and, based upon the evidence, they cannot disprove my statement."

For the first time, Jenkins looked worried. "Your honor," he said, "I ask to reopen my case and—"

"Oh no, judge," I interrupted, "they rested. Moreover, there was no lab technician on the witness list they provided. I prepared my entire case on this point. To allow them to reopen their case would be beyond prejudicial."

Marino had clearly had enough. He waved his hands almost frantically. "Both of you stop talking," he ordered. "The prosecutor's request to reopen the case is denied."

He then looked at me. "As for you," he said accusingly, "I don't like your tone, but you are correct. The prosecution has failed to prove whether their exhibit is cocaine or something else. The charges are dismissed and the defendant is free to go."

He banged his gavel loudly and stood up so quickly, his bailiff forgot to even ask for everyone to stand. As a result, nobody did and the judge simply left.

I walked back to the table and Jose looked at me in confusion. "I fucking won?" he asked.

"Yes, Jose," I answered, "we won."

"Holy shit," he replied with a smile. "I never won in court before. Thanks, man."

"You're welcome, Jose. Now do me a favor. Get a job and stop selling fucking drugs."

Jose paused for a moment before answering, "I will try, sir." I knew damn well that he would be back.

With that, the guards took him back to the holding cell. He would need to be returned to the county jail and processed before he was released.

I picked up my file and turned toward the audience. Becky and Casey were already heading toward me. I took two steps and Becky grabbed me in a hug.

"You were absolutely brilliant," she said, continuing to hug me. "You won without even asking a question."

I looked at Casey, who was smiling as well.

"Not too shabby, huh?" I asked.

"You didn't suck," she said sarcastically before breaking into a big smile. "I guess I can keep working for you."

It might have been the nicest thing she had ever said to me.

15

Outside the courthouse, I collapsed. I had been fighting the dizziness and headache throughout the trial. Just as I stepped off the sidewalk toward the street, it finally overcame me. My right foot slid out from under me and I fell forward and to the right. I landed on the hood of an old gray Plymouth with a thud.

Becky and Casey raced over and helped me up, each woman grabbing an arm. I tried to assure them that I was okay, but neither one was buying it. I asked to go to the office, but there was no arguing with them. They informed me that I was being taken home to rest. I knew better than to argue with Casey. What surprised me was how adamant Becky was. Neither woman was taking no for an answer. I reluctantly agreed on condition that Casey drove like a normal person. She said something about me being a wimp as I climbed into the passenger seat. Becky just smiled before closing my door and heading to her own car to follow.

As we started the journey to my home, Casey's sarcastic wit quickly returned. "At least you fell on an old piece of shit instead of one of the lawyers' BMWs or Mercedes."

"Are you kidding?" I answered. "That car was a classic. That was a 1973 Plymouth Scamp."

Casey laughed derisively. "Looks like 1973 was the last time it was washed," she retorted.

I kept arguing the point. "Those cars had a slant six engine and were always easy to work on," I protested. "Eddie Astorino had one a lot like that when we were in high school."

"If Eddie had it," she said mockingly, "he probably got drunk and crashed it."

I knew she was not going to be convinced, so I let it go.

When we finally got into my home, I changed into pajamas and got into bed. A few minutes later, both women came into my bedroom.

"I'm heading back to the office, Connor," Casey said. "After all, someone needs to get some work done."

I smiled. "Maybe I'll be by later this afternoon," I answered.

"Oh, no," Becky interjected, "you're not going anywhere. You're going to rest."

"Yes, ma'am," I replied sarcastically.

Casey smirked before saying, "If anything comes up, I'll call. Besides, I could use some peace and quiet for once."

She said her goodbyes and left. I turned in my bed to face Becky. "Well, I guess we will have to reschedule our lunch date."

"Nonsense," she said with a serious face. "You just get some sleep and I'll make our lunch. We'll just eat here."

I almost laughed. "I have virtually no food here," I said.

"I noticed," she answered almost immediately. "I saw a small market down at the bottom of the hill. I'm sure they will have something."

I felt almost embarrassed. "You don't have to do my shopping, Becky. Once I am—"

"Enough," she ordered, her face half serious and half smiling. "You are in bed with a concussion because you were helping me with my asshole ex-husband. The least I can do is make you lunch."

As she stood over me with her finger pointed, I found that I had nothing to say. It had been a long time since I had someone looking out for me. I liked it. I just threw her a mock salute and pulled the covers up.

She smiled softly, before leaning down and kissing me on my cheek. As she was moving away from me, we both paused as we stared into each other's eyes. I felt drawn to her in a way I had not experienced for a long time. We just looked at each other for what seemed like forever. Then, without a word, she smiled and walked out of the room.

I lay there for a few minutes, thinking. This past week, I had two fights with a large and very angry ex-football player, a concussion, a swollen eye, a misdemeanor trial victory, a major murder case, and a serial killer returned from the past. It had certainly been overwhelming.

Yet none of these things were consuming my thoughts more than Becky Foster. If someone had told me a week ago that I would have a beautiful woman in my home preparing me lunch, I would have told him they were certifiably crazy. Yet, here she was.

I felt more than a little guilty. I knew what I was feeling toward her. I had avoided even thinking about it. I was torn between my love for Melissa and my more than passing interest in Becky. It had been ten years. I would always love Melissa, but couldn't help feeling that by allowing myself to care for another woman, I was somehow betraying her and what we had. I also knew that Melissa would want me to be happy. It was one thing to start handling cases in County Court again. Starting a new relationship with a woman was something else entirely.

I must have fallen asleep because the next thing I knew, there was a knock at my bedroom door. I was startled and looked up to see Becky coming in carrying a tray. I sat up and she placed it on my lap.

I was expecting a sandwich, maybe even a grilled cheese, with some soup. What I got instead was a delicious-looking grilled chicken salad with chopped apples, walnuts, and crumbled cheese.

"Wow," I said, "where did you find that?"

"Found?" she asked, seeming almost insulted. "That's a home-cooked meal, buddy."

I realized that I had screwed up. "My apologies," I answered. "I am looking forward to eating it after I take my foot out of my mouth."

She smiled, but said nothing. I realized she was waiting for me to try it. I grabbed my fork and took a bite of the chicken. It was wonderful. She had used a combination of spices that really brought out the flavor of the meat without overwhelming it.

I had taken four or five bites before realizing that I had not said anything. I looked up and saw Becky just waiting.

"I take it you like it?" she asked.

"Absolutely delicious," I answered.

She smiled in appreciation, got up, and left. She returned about a minute later with her own tray of food. She sat down in a chair near my bed and began to eat. We said little. I was very hungry and concentrated on devouring the tasty food.

When we finished our meal, she started collecting the plates and trays. She took them out of the room and returned a few minutes later. "How are you feeling?" she asked.

My headache was still there, but nowhere near as painful as it had been. My nausea was finally gone as well. "Not too bad," I said. "In a day or two, I should be ready to beat up some more of your old boyfriends."

My joke fell flat. She said nothing, but sat down next to me on my bed. The look on her face was very serious. "I didn't come to you looking for you to get into fights," she said, her eyes beginning to glisten, "and certainly not for you to get hurt." She paused, and ran her finger gently over my swollen eye before continuing. "I just didn't know where else to turn."

Tears started streaming down her face. She tried to speak again, but couldn't. She got up suddenly and bolted from the room.

I got out of bed and went after her. I felt slightly dizzy, but did not let it slow me down. I caught up to her in the living room. She was looking out the picture window. Her shoulders were shaking with her sobs.

I placed my hands on her shoulders and lightly turned her around to face me. She flushed with embarrassment. "I'm sorry," she started to say, but I cut her right off.

"There's nothing to be sorry about. I knew when I agreed to help you that Matt and I might have to fight."

"I knew he might get violent," she continued. "I just thought that you could do something as a lawyer to stop him. I didn't want you to fight him."

"I was kind of hoping we would," I answered, realizing I had said too much. Becky picked right up on what I said.

"You wanted to fight him?" she asked. "Why on earth would you want to fight such a big guy?"

Now I was the one who was embarrassed. In my mind, I chided myself for being so foolish. "Well," I stammered, "I just never liked that asshole. He needed a beating."

Becky wasn't buying it. "I agree that he's an asshole," she said, "but that's not enough to pick a fight with him."

"I didn't pick a fight with him," I insisted. "I tried talking with him and he came after me with a wrench."

"But once he did that?" Becky asked.

"Then I threw him into a pile of hubcaps and stood on his throat," I said.

She started laughing. "So that's what you meant when you said you hubcapped him," she said, continuing to laugh.

I nodded. She stopped laughing and that serious look returned to her face. "Okay, so he started the fight. But that doesn't explain why you wanted to beat him up. Once he gave you the excuse, you didn't hesitate. I want to know why."

I hesitated. This was not something I wanted to talk about. I had been pressured many times by judges and other lawyers. That was never a problem. Responding to them was easy. *Why is it so hard to resist this woman,* I wondered.

"What did you ever see in that loser anyway?" I asked, trying to change the subject.

"What?" she replied, seemingly confused. "What's that got to do with it?"

"You always went for jackasses like him," I accused. "If they were big dumb jocks, they ended up being your boyfriends."

Becky's face showed a combination of anger and surprise, but I just kept going. "I never understood why you went out with losers like him. You deserved so much better."

She did not initially respond. After a moment, she finally answered, "I guess the person I really liked never asked me out."

She let her words linger for a while before she spoke again. "I answered your question. Now you need to answer mine. Why did you want to fight Matt so badly?"

All I wanted to do was ask about what she had just said. The person she really liked? Who was she talking about? She was the most attractive and popular girl in school, and just about every guy had asked her out.

As much as I wanted to ask her for details, the look on her face made it quite clear that she would accept nothing but a direct answer to her question.

"I know he slapped you around," I said. "You deserved better than that."

"You wanted to fight him because he hit me?" she asked.

"Right."

"But why?" she asked persistently.

"Because you deserved better," I said again.

She took a step forward and got right in my face. "Answer my question," she demanded. "Why did you want to fight him?"

When I paused, my frustration growing rapidly, she continued, "And don't you dare say that I deserved better."

"Well, you did," I said, beginning to lose my composure. "The idea of that piece of garbage putting his hands on you made me furious."

"Why?" she insisted, looking me straight in the eyes.

"Because I care about you," I blurted out, my defenses finally breaking apart. "I've always cared about you, ever since we were kids, but you never wanted me. You only wanted those big stupid jocks."

Becky smiled broadly, but this just seemed to pour fuel on my growing fire. She had pressured me into revealing something I preferred to keep to myself, and she found it funny. I was about to say something when she spoke again.

"You jackass," she said, starting to laugh.

Nothing could have prepared me for that response.

"Jackass?" I asked. "I'm a jackass for caring about you?"

"No," Becky said, a warm yet sad expression appearing on her face. "You're a jackass because the one I really wanted to be with was you."

I just stood there stunned. I tried to speak, but found I had no words.

"I went out with those jerks," Becky said, breaking the tense silence, "because you, the guy I was in love with, never asked me out."

"You were in love with me?" I asked, almost not believing the words as I said them.

"For as long as I can remember," she said, not breaking her stare, "but you never seemed to be interested. Then you left for college. When Matt asked me to marry him, I wasn't sure you were ever coming back, so I said yes."

We both stood quietly looking at each other.

"I had no idea you felt that way, Becky," I offered. "I wish I had known."

I was going to say something else, but the words caught in my throat as I found myself lost in Becky's alluring brown eyes. The world was silent and it was as if nothing else existed.

Then Becky moved in closer and kissed me. I could feel the soft caress of her lips and smell the sweetness of her perfume. Instead of the guilt I had experienced earlier, this time I felt nothing but desire. I slid my hand into her hair, pulled her close, and kept on kissing her.

16

I awoke a couple of hours later. For a second, I was not sure where I was or how I got there. It all came back to me when Becky stirred slightly. She was lying on my left side with her head on my chest. She opened her eyes and smiled. "Hi, there," she said, in a voice both sexy and sleepy at the same time.

I just stared at her, almost in disbelief. Here I was, lying in bed with Becky Foster, both of us naked as the day we were born. It was almost surreal. I had always believed that once Melissa died, I was never going to be with anyone else. It had always seemed impossible. Yet, here I was with a woman I had known since childhood and had loved long before I ever even met Melissa.

Becky pulled herself on top of me, her breasts sliding across my chest. "So," she said seductively, "the great lawyer is at a loss for words?"

Before I could come up with a snappy reply, she kissed me hard and with an obvious intent. I kissed her and ran my hands down her back until they reached her behind. She groaned when I cupped her cheeks and pulled her forward. She adjusted her hips slightly and took me inside her. We made love again.

When we finished, she moved back to my side and began casually running her fingertips across my chest. We lay there quietly for a long time.

"Can I ask you something, Connor?" Becky asked, breaking the silence.

"Sure," I said.

She paused for a moment as she crafted her question in her head. "It's about your fight with Matt."

"After what we just did, you want to talk about Matt Jordan?" I asked incredulously.

"No, no," she answered, laughing nervously. "Nothing like that. I just don't understand how you beat him. He's almost six inches taller than you and outweighs you by eighty or ninety pounds."

I really had no desire to talk about the fight, but knew she would keep pushing until I answered her directly. "I used judo," I finally said.

"You mean like Bruce Lee in the movies?" she asked.

"No, nothing like that," I said. "That's a form of karate. I used judo."

"I don't understand," she replied. "What's the difference?"

"Judo involves using your opponent's size and strength against him."

"But how do you throw someone so big?" she asked.

"Kuzushi," I answered.

"Ku who shi?" Becky asked, starting to giggle.

"Kuzushi," I corrected. "It's a Japanese term. It means getting your opponent off balance. If you get him off balance, he becomes easy to throw."

"So you got Matt off balance?" she asked, sounding not quite convinced.

"Right," I said. "He lunged at me with a wrench trying to hit me. When he did, he was off balance and easier to throw. You understand?"

"Sort of," Becky said. "It almost sounds like he got himself off balance and you took advantage of it."

"Exactly," I responded. "When a bigger opponent comes at you with force, if you resist with force, the bigger and stronger man usually wins. But if you give way to his forceful attack—"

"The bigger guy goes flying into a pile of hubcaps." Becky laughed, finishing my sentence for me.

"Something like that," I replied.

She was quiet for a minute before speaking again. "Do you think you could teach me?" she asked.

This was not something I expected. I'd never taught judo or even really considered it. It was an interesting idea, though. I'd been thinking about going back to my old dojo and resuming my judo workouts, especially after the last few days.

"I guess I could," I replied. "I'm a Nidan."

"Nidan?" she asked.

"Sorry," I said quickly, "Nidan is a second-degree black belt."

"That makes you a judo master?" she asked in a voice that seemed slightly sarcastic, yet still serious.

"No, I'm not a master or expert," I replied.

I noticed the expression on Becky's face fall slightly. She was obviously disappointed with my answer.

"But," I continued, "I am pretty good."

Becky's smile returned. Her smile was not something easily described. It was something that made you feel like being covered with a warm blanket on a cold night. You just want to hold onto it and never move.

We said nothing for the next minute or two. Finally, Becky broke the silence.

"I'd really like to learn," she said. "Maybe if I'd known judo, Matt wouldn't have been able to..." Her voice trailed off and she looked away, trying to hide the pain I had already seen in her eyes.

I put my arms around her and pulled her close. She was trying very hard not to cry even though her face was a mask of emotion. I put my index finger under her chin and lifted her face gently so I could look at her directly. "You are perfectly safe with me," I said, trying to assure her, "but if you really want to learn judo, I'll take you to the place where I used to train."

Her eyes glistened slightly as she forced a smile. "My hero," she said softly, before embracing me tightly. I just held her, occasionally stroking her long, soft hair.

As the minutes passed, my mind wandered, trying to figure out exactly how I had gone from lying in a hospital bed in the morning to lying in my own bed holding a beautiful woman in just a matter of hours. I wondered if maybe I was actually still in the hospital and everything else was a delusional fantasy brought on by my concussion. That seemed more plausible to me than the reality.

I was still considering this when Becky sat up suddenly, startling me.

"What time is it?" she asked in a panicked voice.

I looked over at my clock radio before answering. "It's about ten minutes to three. Why?"

"Oh my God," she said, throwing back the covers and leaping to her feet. "I'm going to be late for work. Can I use your shower?"

I barely had time to nod as she grabbed her clothes in a bundle and walked past me toward the bathroom. I hated to see her leave my bed, but certainly enjoyed the view as she did.

I heard the shower turn on and decided to get up too. As I stood, I felt some dizziness and nausea. It was a not-so-subtle reminder of the monstrous punches Matt Jordan had landed on my face and head. I grabbed a robe and wrapped it around me before putting on slippers.

I was about to sit down in the kitchen when the bathroom door burst open and Becky hurried out. She was fully dressed now. She grabbed her purse and came straight to the kitchen. She grabbed a glass from the drying rack next to the sink and moved toward the refrigerator.

"So," I began, trying to think of something to say. It had been easy to talk while we were in bed. Now it seemed difficult. Eventually, I blurted out, "Where do you work anyway?"

She yanked open the fridge and pulled out a carton of orange juice. She must have bought it because I know I never did. As she poured herself a glass, she answered, "I am the hostess at the Medallion on the four-to-eleven shift."

The Medallion was the closest thing Rockfield had to a gourmet restaurant. They served French food mostly. The owner had come to Rockfield almost twelve years ago looking to bring some culture to our small rural community. I tried the place once. The food was good, though perhaps not worth the price he charged.

Becky drank her juice in one long gulp and then put her glass in the sink. She pulled out her keys and looked back at me. "You going to be okay while I'm gone?" she asked.

"I'm fine, Becky," I said. "Go ahead to work. I'll manage."

She came over to me, embraced me, and then kissed me. She opened the door and started walking through before stopping and looking back at me. She gave me a stern look and pointed her finger at me accusingly. "You take it easy and rest. You hear me?"

I walked over to her, holding up my hands in mock surrender. "Yes, warden," I replied sarcastically. She gave me that incredible smile, kissed me tenderly, and then walked off the porch.

I stood in the doorway until she started her car and drove away. When her car disappeared from my sight, I went back into my house and closed the door.

~

Charles Edward Duncan was still in his car. It had been simple to follow Phelan from the courthouse back to his home. He had observed carefully as two women helped Connor into his house. His evil adversary had seemed weak and vulnerable, but Duncan knew that this was just a ruse, a trap set for him. He was too clever to fall for the evil one's snare.

He watched as one of the women came back out of the house about ten minutes later and drove away. He had considered following her. The woman had pretty tattoos on her shoulder and neck. He envisioned sliding his arms around her and squeezing until her last breath rattled out. The release from that would be glorious. He groaned almost in ecstasy as he fantasized about the kill.

It was almost too tempting to resist, but he took every bit of inner strength he could muster to push his thoughts back into the recesses of his mind. Now was not the time. He had to focus. He had to defeat Phelan, the cursed talisman. If he did not, he would be driven into the Catskill Mountains to hunt for animals to stifle his unrelenting pain. He would once again become an inhuman monster. He would wait.

Hours passed and still he waited. As he did, the searing white-hot pain surged within him just below the surface. He had to keep it contained. He was not sure just how much longer he could last before he would be forced to kill and experience relief or be consumed by the fiery furnace within his body.

As the minutes passed, Duncan would occasionally look over to the passenger seat. There on the seat was the glinting blade of his hunting knife. This was the weapon he would use to cut off Connor Phelan's head after he squeezed every last breath out of him. He would take his head and put it in his display with all the clothes he had taken from the women he had killed. Touching these clothes always reminded Duncan of the moment of release after his kill. What pleasure he would have when he touched the severed head of the talisman!

He was as sure as he had ever been of anything in his life. It would be the killing of Phelan and the keeping of his enemy's head that would end his pain once and for all.

As he contemplated such things, the pain occasionally surged so intensely that he nearly shrieked in agony. Periodically, his hands trembled, his body stiffened and twisted, and cold sweat ran down his face.

His agony was interrupted when the front door of the evil one's home opened. He sat straight up and focused all his energy. He saw the second woman, the pretty blonde. She came out of the house, paused in the doorway, and turned back. She pointed her finger at someone, almost as if she were chastising him.

Then he saw him. Connor Phelan stepped into the doorway, his hands raised in the air. Whatever this woman had said, the evil one was surrendering himself to her. She had control over him. Duncan sat transfixed as the woman kissed Phelan before walking to her car and driving away.

Phelan, the evil talisman, just stood there. He did not move at all until the blonde got in her car and drove away. Even when she was gone, Phelan lingered for a moment. Finally, he went back into the house.

Duncan knew immediately that he had found his opportunity, the weakness of his opponent that he could exploit. His arms tingled with excitement as his mind raced. He knew exactly how he could defeat the evil one and extinguish the fire within once and for all.

He started his car and drove away. There were preparations to make, but the next time he encountered the evil one, he would kill him. *Most important,* Duncan thought, *there is absolutely nothing Connor Phelan can do to stop it.*

17

After Becky left, I decided to take a shower. As the hot water and soap ran down my body and into the drain, I thought about what had happened over the previous few hours.

Making love to Becky had been wonderful. When it had happened and even afterwards as I held her, I had no doubts that this was exactly what I wanted. Now that she was gone, though, doubt began to creep in.

My thoughts went to Melissa, my wife and mother of my unborn son. We had pledged to spend our lives together. We had planned to have two children, a son and a daughter. We were going to share our lives, our careers, and the joy of our family together. We had talked about grandchildren and eventually retiring to either Florida or the Carolinas when we got old. All of that had been ripped away in an instant.

I felt torn. I was being pulled in two completely different directions. On one side was Becky. It was an opportunity to start a new relationship, a new life. We were both forty years old, so a family might not be in the cards, though maybe it was possible. She already had a daughter who was a freshman in college. Would she want another child?

On the other side was the life I had and had planned with Melissa. I felt as though I had betrayed her. I had never even considered being unfaithful. I had never even been tempted. I knew that the bonds of marriage ended when she died. Making love to Becky was not cheating. Why did it feel as if I had?

I knew in my heart that Melissa would want me to move on. I could almost hear her speaking in my mind and saying, *It's been ten years, you big dope. What are you waiting for?*

These thoughts and contradictions went round and round in my head, along with the pain from my concussion, until I was jolted back to reality by cold water. I must have lost track of time and used up all the hot water. I quickly turned off the shower and grabbed a towel.

I made my way into my bedroom and started getting dressed. I was halfway dressed and about to put on a shirt when the phone started ringing. My hello was greeted by the voice of Dom Bryce. "Hey handsome," he said, "you feeling any better?"

"Actually," I answered, "I think I have felt better in the last few hours than I have in a very long time."

"Well," he said, not missing a beat, "some of those pain pills they give you can make a man feel pretty good. Just be careful, though, they can also mess with your head."

"No doubt," I said, with a big smile on my face before changing the subject. "What's up, boss? Clancy give us anything?"

"Not really," he said. "That old drunk didn't really know much."

"He must have seen something," I protested.

"Hey, I want this killer worse than you do," Dom replied, "but he claims he never even saw the body. He just grabbed what he could in the bedroom and got out of there. It was late at night and there was nobody around."

"Shit," I said. "He didn't see another person at all that night? I was sure that Clancy would've seen something."

"He didn't see anyone around the house," Dom said. "In fact, he saw only one person the entire night, but didn't get a good look. Just a white guy in an old car."

"Where did he see this guy?" I asked.

"About a quarter mile from the house. Clancy was driving up the hill toward the house and the guy passed him going the other way––"

"That was probably the killer," I interrupted, surprised Dom had not considered this.

"I already thought of that, pal, and you're probably right," Dom continued. "The problem is that Clancy didn't get a plate number and the only thing he could say about the driver was that he was white. Can't even give an age."

This was damn frustrating. Clancy had probably seen the Rockfield Strangler, but could not give us anything of substance.

"Dom, you told me once that you sometimes use techniques to relax a witness so they can recall details," I offered.

"I tried that, Connor," he interjected. "I got some vague information on the car, but not the driver."

"The fucker couldn't even give you hair color or anything?" I asked.

"Nope," Dom answered, frustrated, "he couldn't even tell me what color shirt the driver was wearing. Nothing."

"Son of a bitch," I swore. "Fat load of good this witness is going to be."

"Yeah," Dom said, "The most I could get from him was a white guy driving a Dodge Dart from the early seventies."

Dom's words hit me like a ton of bricks. "What did you just say?" I asked.

"I said he just saw a white guy."

"No, no, not the driver," I said, "the car. What did he say about the car?"

"He said it was a Dodge Dart from the early seventies," Dom repeated. "So what?"

I suddenly remembered my fall in front of the courthouse. It ran through my mind almost in slow motion. I could see the old gray car I landed on. Casey's words reverberated in my head: *At least you fell on an old piece of shit.*

As I realized what it all likely meant, a cold shiver ran up and down my spine. "Dom, did he tell you what color it was? Was it gray?"

"Yeah," Dom replied, "how did you—"

"Did you run a DMV check yet?" I interrupted.

"No, not yet," Dom responded. "I was going to, but haven't had time yet. I only just got out of the interview room at the jail."

"We have to do this right away, Dom. No time to lose."

"Okay," Dom said, "I'll head to the main station. The lieutenant on shift over there is an old friend of mine. I'll have him give me a listing of every Dodge Dart in the area from the 1970s—"

"Dom, it's not a Dodge Dart," I interrupted. "It's a '73 Plymouth Scamp."

"How the fuck could you possibly know that?" Dom demanded. "Clancy said it was a Dodge."

I was not prepared to share what I now knew in my gut to be true. The car I had fallen on several hours ago was the same car Bob Clancy saw on the night of the murder. I had no definitive proof, but I was sure as I could be about anything.

"The Dodge Dart and Plymouth Scamp were sister cars. They looked almost exactly alike," I said. Dom tried to say something, but I cut him right off. "Also, pull every piece of video footage you can possibly find from the night of the murder. If we can find that car, we find the Strangler."

"I already did that," Dom replied. "Like I told you, it's not my first rodeo. We should have footage available to review later tonight. How about I come by with the footage and some beer around nine?"

"Include some pizza and it's a deal, boss," I agreed.

"Connor?" Dom asked, a strong note of concern in his voice. "Are you sure about it being a Plymouth? Clancy insisted it was a Dodge."

"Trust me, boss. Besides, since when do you take the word of a drunk anyway?" I asked. "Just let me know if you get anything."

I hung up before he could even answer. My mind was spinning and my thoughts racing. If I was right—and I was sure I was—then there could be only two possible conclusions. If the car Clancy saw that night was the same '73 Plymouth at the courthouse, then either it was the biggest coincidence of all time, or the Rockfield Strangler was keeping a close eye on my investigation and me. I needed to be careful.

That night, true to his word, Dom Bryce showed up at nine o'clock on the button. I opened the door and he walked in carrying a cardboard box with a pizza and a six-pack of beer resting on top.

"Special delivery," he announced.

I took the beer and pizza from him and brought it into the living room. Dom went right to the television. He set down his box and pulled out a DVD. As he put it into the player, I cracked open two beers and opened the pizza box.

One side of the pizza looked great with large sliced meatballs. The other half was covered in mushrooms, onions, black olives, and anchovies. It looked and smelled horrible.

"Holy shit, Dom," I protested, "how can you eat that garbage?"

He laughed. "Don't knock it till you try it, kid. It's good. It'll put hair on your ass."

I took another look at the swill on his half of the pizza. "Looks like they already put ass hair on it."

Dom frowned. "You just eat your half and leave the good stuff for me."

I grabbed a beer and two slices of meatball pizza and sat down in my chair to eat. As we ate and drank, Dom started the DVD player. We watched numerous pieces of footage from ATM machines, stores, and parking lots. There was nothing of consequence.

The final footage was a series of digital photographs from a traffic light camera about a mile from the Coleman home. There were three pictures. The first two were SUVs. The final picture showed the side of a gray Plymouth. I sat right up. It looked like the same car I fell on at the courthouse.

"I think that's it," I said excitedly. "Can we get the plate number?"

"No," Dom said, shaking his head, "fucking piece of shit camera only got a side shot in the intersection."

I shook my head in exasperation. "You have anything else?" I asked.

Dom tossed me a folder. Inside was a computer printout. I scanned it quickly.

"That there," Dom announced, "is a list of all 1973 Plymouth Scamps and Dodge Darts registered in Linton County. As well as the four counties to the north, east, south, and west. There are 153 of them."

"I don't care about the Darts," I insisted. "How many Plymouths are there?"

"Forty-six," he answered, "but how do you—"

"And how many of the forty-six are gray?" I asked, cutting him off and ignoring his planned question.

"None," he replied to my shock.

"That can't be right," I replied.

"I checked it out. Those cars were not offered in gray in 1973," Dom advised.

"But I saw it and it was gray," I insisted.

"I'm a step ahead of you, kid," Dom said with an annoying smirk on his face. "I checked with a buddy of mine who really knows cars. He said that the car was probably sky blue when it was new, but once it was no longer shiny, it looks gray, almost like primer."

"Okay, Sherlock," I said sarcastically, "how many in your record were sky blue?"

Dom looked at his notes again. "Four," he finally said, "assuming none have been painted that color and not reported."

"Run all their names for me and see if they have any criminal records or interesting backgrounds."

Dom just stared at me for a moment. It was obvious that he was pissed off. After another few seconds of him just staring, I had enough.

"What?" I asked.

"You still haven't told me how you know it's a Plymouth and not a Dodge," he said.

"Call it a hunch," I replied.

"Fuck that noise," Dom answered immediately. "If I'm going to spend half the night digging up dirt on these four people, I want to know fucking why."

"Fine," I answered, and told him about falling on the gray Plymouth after court on Friday.

Dom was incredulous. "That's your fucking proof?" he yelled. "Just because you fell on some fucking jalopy, you think it's some great piece of evidence?"

This was the reaction I had expected. "He's following our

investigation, Dom, I know it," I persisted. "It makes perfect sense."

Dom shook his head. "You're grasping at fucking straws," he finally said.

"No!" I hollered back. "I don't think it's a coincidence that Clancy saw a gray Plymouth that night and then the same car or type of car is at the courthouse."

"He said it was a Dodge!" Dom screamed back.

"He's a drunk," I countered. "He doesn't know the fucking difference."

"And you're a lawyer, not a fucking car mechanic!" he screamed again. "Plus from that lousy side picture, it's hard to even tell the difference. This is a wild fucking goose chase."

"Look, boss," I said, "just do me this favor. Run those four names tonight and let me know what you get."

Dom threw his hands in the air in frustration, but I kept pushing. "Do me this favor," I said. "If it turns out to be nothing, I'll buy dinner at any place you want."

"Any place I want?" Dom asked, showing some interest.

"You got it," I answered.

Dom considered it for a moment. "Fine," he said at last.

"Just please don't order any of the shitty fish pizza," I said with a smile.

"Fuck that," Dom said. "If you're buying, it's filet mignon and Dom Pérignon."

I put my hand out and he shook it.

Dom looked at me and laughed before saying, "First bet I ever made that I want to fucking lose."

18

The next morning, I was up even before my alarm clock went off. Adrenaline was racing through me. I knew Dom would have the information on the owners of the four Plymouths. This could be the day the Rockfield Strangler would finally be caught.

In what seemed like moments, I was showered, shaved, and dressed. I hopped into my Cherokee and headed straight to the office. I skipped my usual stop for coffee and a breakfast sandwich. I was far too excited for food.

As I drove past my office and turned into the parking lot, my exuberance turned to anxiety and trepidation. There were at least thirty-five people gathered by my office door. They had microphones, notepads, and television cameras. *Why is the media here?* I wondered.

I pulled into my designated spot and killed the engine. As I got out of the Cherokee, the entire swarm of people started running toward me, screaming my name. I thought something might have happened to Casey or Dom, but that thought was quickly cast aside when I heard the first few questions being shouted at me.

"Mr. Phelan, when did you know the Rockfield Strangler had returned?"

"How long have the police known about the DNA evidence linking this case to the Strangler?"

"Do you know who the Strangler really is yet?"

Somehow, the press was aware of both the DNA evidence and the connection to the old Rockfield Strangler cases. I tried to make sense of this. I knew without even considering it that neither Dom nor Casey would have spilled the beans. Becky knew about the evidence, but I found it nearly impossible to believe that she had told the media.

Who had the motive or desire to leak the information? I tried to consider this, but could not ponder the matter further as the crowd was now encircling me and screaming questions from almost every angle.

I started walking toward the front door of my office. I wanted these people out of my parking lot and away from my car. As I started moving, the mass of humanity followed me. I nearly stepped on two reporters who walked right in front of me.

I hollered out, "No comment!" two or three times, but this made the men and women yell even louder. The sheer volume of their questions echoed inside my head in a not-so-subtle reminder that although I felt better this morning, I was not yet recovered from my concussion.

When I felt the first signs of nausea building, I knew I had to do something. I stopped and raised both hands high over my head.

"Quiet please!" I hollered, as my head started to really hurt. "I will make a brief statement if you will just give me your attention."

This seemed to satisfy the reporters and they stopped screaming. I lowered my hands, grateful for the silence.

"Ladies and gentlemen," I announced in my courtroom

voice, "as special prosecutor, I am looking into all relevant avenues of investigation."

"But what about the Strangler?" a young reporter shouted out. This caused the other reporters to start shouting questions as well.

Not wanting the volume to build back to a crescendo, I again raised my hands and asked for quiet. When they stopped their incessant yammering, I spoke again. "As for your questions about the Rockfield Strangler, I will neither confirm nor deny any possible connections to those cases."

The reporters immediately started grumbling, but I was not going to stick around for another verbal barrage. "I will give my word, however, that the moment I am in a position to discuss details of my investigation, I will hold a press conference and answer all of your questions."

I then walked quickly toward my office door. The reporters gave chase and shouted questions at me. I ignored them and went into my office. One reporter tried to follow me inside. I placed my right hand on his chest and pushed him back far enough so I could close and lock the door.

I had just finished locking the deadbolt when I heard Casey Franklin's voice. "Fucking vultures," she grumbled. "They've been here for over an hour. They asked me questions when I got here. Like I would tell those assholes anything."

"Well, here's the real question," I said. "Who told those clowns about the Strangler?"

"I hope you don't think it was me." Casey's tone made it crystal clear that daring to even consider that possibility would result in very unpleasant consequences.

I smiled. "I know better than that, Case. I never question your loyalty."

"Damn straight," she said, "but I knew coming in this morning that it might be like this."

"You knew the press would be here today?" I was stunned at what she had just said.

"Of course," she answered. "Didn't you?"

"Why would I have had any idea that my office would be swarming with media?"

"You didn't see it, did you?"

"See what?" I demanded. "What the hell are you talking about?"

Casey gave me a look like I had said something colossally stupid. She then walked over to the desk, picked up a newspaper, and brought it to me. "Read it and weep," she said sarcastically as she thrust it into my hands.

It was the morning edition of the *Rockfield Tribune*. I unfolded it and took a look. "EXCLUSIVE: Rockfield Strangler Returns" was the headline.

"Oh shit," I said.

"Read on," Casey said. "It gets better."

"I think I need to sit down first," I said wearily. I walked into my office, sat in my chair, and spread the paper across my desk.

A source inside the County Courthouse confirms that charges of murder against Robert Clancy were dismissed by Special Prosecutor Connor Phelan after DNA evidence was uncovered linking the crime to the infamous Rockfield Strangler.

The Strangler terrorized Rockfield in 1999 and 2000, attacking four women and killing three, before mysteriously disappearing.

I stopped reading. I knew eventually this media circus was going to happen. I had just hoped to keep things quiet for a little longer. Now the secret was out. Even worse, if the Strangler saw this—and he almost certainly would—he might go back into hiding. Whoever leaked this information had potentially caused real damage to the investigation.

I was about to resume reading when Casey called out from her desk. "Connor, Old Iron Girdle on line two."

Just what I need, I thought. Putting the paper aside, I picked up the phone. "Connor Phelan," I announced.

"Mr. Phelan," Ethel Bollenbacher's stern voice replied, "hold for Judge Hardy."

I said nothing and merely waited. A moment later, John J. Hardy was on the line. He was angry and made no attempt to hide it. "Have you seen the fucking paper, Connor?" he asked.

"I have, judge," I said. I knew from experience that if Hardy was swearing, it was best to not say very much.

"I can't believe that fucking cocksucker leaked it," he raged. "I'll have his fucking head."

I knew instinctively who he was talking about. There really was only one man with any motive to leak the information and hurt the case. "Worthington," I said flatly.

"Of course Worthington!" Hardy shouted back. "I knew as soon as I saw who wrote the article."

I took a quick glance at the paper. The article had been written by Harry Wagner, the longest-serving reporter at the *Tribune*. He had been covering the news in Rockfield for nearly fifty years.

"How does the story being written by Harry prove it was Worthington?" I asked.

"Isn't that how you knew it was that scumbag?" Hardy asked.

"No," I answered, "I just figured he was the one with the motive. He was pissed that you allowed me to keep the case, so he is trying to sabotage it."

"That's his fucking plan!" Hardy yelled. "But Wagner clinches it for me."

"How so?"

"Harry always had the inside track with the district attorney's office going back even before I had the job," Hardy said. "He is the one reporter that everyone in the office trusts. He always gets it right and he never reveals a source."

"Well, judge," I continued, "we both know it's Worthington, but have no real reliable proof to accuse him."

"If we did," Hardy fumed, "I'd haul his ass in here and send him to the county lockup for contempt."

I thought for a minute before speaking. "John, can you do me a favor on this one?"

Hardy paused momentarily before saying, "What is it, my boy?"

"Don't let Worthington know that we suspect him," I said. "I'll deal with him in my own time and it will be better if he doesn't know it's coming."

Hardy grunted. It was a grunt of both laughter and derision. "What do you have in mind, son?" the judge asked.

"I'm not sure just yet," I said, "but I'll come up with something, and it's probably better that you don't know."

Hardy seemed to consider this for a moment or two before responding. "All right," he finally said, "Mum's the word... for now."

"Thanks, judge," I said, and we ended the call without another word.

I started looking through the newspaper again to see if there were any other surprises. There were none. Apparently, the only thing given to Harry Wagner was the DNA test clearing Clancy and implicating the Strangler. It was bad, but not a total disaster.

I had just finished folding up the paper when I heard loud knocking on our back door and Dom Bryce's voice booming from outside. "Open the damn door, Casey!" he roared. I could also now hear the flock of reporters yelling questions at Dom.

I got up from my desk and quickly walked toward the commotion. Casey was at the back door with her hands near the lock. She had a big smile on her face.

From the other side of the door, I could hear the reporters continuing to scream questions.

"Get away from me!" Dom yelled back to them. A moment later, he yelled, "Casey, open the goddamn door!"

Casey was laughing. "Say pretty please," she said mockingly, clearly enjoying herself.

"Casey," I yelled out, "open the door!"

She smirked, but did as she was told. Dom Bryce immediately came through the door carrying two manila envelopes, his cowboy hat barely clinging to his head. He and Casey closed and locked the door as the reporters continued to shout questions.

Dom said angrily to Casey, "What's the big idea leaving me locked out there with those animals?"

"I thought you'd feel right at home," she answered, walking back to her desk.

"Now see here," Dom yelled, "you've got one hell of a nerve!"

Casey ignored him and sat down. She then looked directly at me. "Mr. Wonderful to see you, Connor."

Bryce was not amused. He pointed his finger at her and said, "You got a bad attitude and a lot of sass, little lady. Someone ought to put you over their knee and wallop your hiney."

Casey immediately stood up. "It sure as hell ain't going to be you," she challenged. "You ain't man enough."

Before things got further out of hand, I intervened. "Okay, enough, both of you!" I shouted. "It's bad enough we got a raving mob of reporters at our door. I don't need World War Three in here. My head hurts enough as it is."

They both tried to argue their points, but I cut them off. "You," I said sternly, pointing at Dom, "in my office."

Dom said nothing, but glared at Casey as he went into my office. "And you," I said to Casey, trying to be stern but breaking into a big smile, "stop pushing his buttons."

As I walked back into my office, I heard Casey say, "I gotta have some fun around here."

I looked back at her. "Dom's right about one thing."

"What's that?"

"You do have a lot of sass."

She chuckled slightly. I just smiled and closed my office door.

19

My door wasn't closed two seconds before Dom started back up.

"You've got to do something about that girl, Connor!" he bellowed. "She's got a real attitude problem. I ought to—"

"Cool your jets, pal," I interrupted. "You're not making things any better by threatening to spank her."

"She sure needs it!" Dom yelled back.

I held up my hands to signal him to stop. "Okay, enough!" I shouted. "Let's get to business."

Dom continued grumbling under his breath as he took off his hat and flung it on the empty chair next to him. Then he tossed the first manila envelope on my desk.

"What's this?" I asked as I opened it and pulled out some papers.

"That is the information about the owners of the four Plymouths," Dom answered. "There's registrations, criminal history, and background information."

"And what's in the other envelope?" I asked.

"Same thing," Dom answered. "It's my copy."

I looked down and started reading through the documents.

"You can forget about the first two people," Dom continued.

"And why is that?" I asked, still reading.

"Well, the first car is owned by an eighty-three-year-old widow over in Catskill," Dom said. "She drives it to church and maybe the market. Not likely that old biddy is choking people out."

"Okay, we can scratch Granny off the list," I conceded. "Why is the second person not a suspect?"

"Michael Shields, from right here in Rockfield," Dom said. "He bought the car a year ago and is trying to fix it up. The car is in his garage and doesn't run. He's also only twenty-two years old."

"Well, scratch him off the list too," I said, "unless he was strangling women at the age of three or four."

I moved through the papers to the information on suspect number three. The third owner was Tim Clayton.

"What about Clayton?" I asked.

"I think this may be our guy, Connor," Dom said, sitting upright. "He's about the right age and he's got a criminal record."

I quickly glanced at his rap sheet. Before I could finish reading, Dom was on his feet pleading his case. "He's fifty-two. The age fits," he said.

"True enough," I said, "tell me about his record." I figured since Dom had already reviewed everything and would just keep talking while I was trying to read, I would be better off just listening to him.

"He was busted for possessing drugs when he was nineteen," Dom offered, "and later he was drinking and driving. Then, to top it off, he was arrested for a felony assault."

At that moment, my door opened and Casey walked in. She was holding two coffee cups. She placed the first one in front of me. "Cream and one sugar," she said, "just the way you like it."

I picked it up and had a sip. It really hit the spot.

"I like my coffee black, honey," Dom said reaching out his hand.

Casey smiled broadly, took a big sip from the cup, and said, "Me too," before walking out of the room.

I almost choked on my coffee from laughing. Dom was not amused. He followed right after her. "I want some coffee too," he complained.

"Coffee is right upstairs in the kitchen," Casey replied. "Help yourself."

I laughed again when I heard Dom walking up the stairs saying something about kids not having respect for their elders.

I decided to take that moment to look through the documents more closely. Although what Dom had told me about Tim Clayton was true, it did not tell the whole story.

The so-called drug bust was actually a charge of unlawful possession of marijuana. The arrest sheet was there. It revealed that Tim had been caught late one Saturday night smoking a joint. The charge was eventually dismissed.

He had been stopped for driving while intoxicated a year later. The arresting officer's affidavit showed that Tim's blood alcohol content was slightly over the legal limit. The matter resolved a month later when Clayton pleaded guilty to a lesser charge and paid a fine.

The assault occurred when Tim was twenty-two. He had been arrested along with fourteen other guys after a fight broke out at a strip club that used to exist on the outskirts of town. Clayton's charge was a felony because he apparently hit someone over the head with a beer bottle. He later pleaded guilty to misdemeanor assault and did thirty days in the county jail.

I had just finished reading the arresting officer's report on the bar fight when Dom came back holding a large mug of coffee. He left the door open before sitting down and putting his feet up on the adjoining chair, right next to his hat.

"So, what do you think?" he asked.

"I'm not so sure he's our guy," I answered. "He raised some hell as a kid, but drinking, smoking grass, and fighting over some strippers doesn't point to murder."

"More likely him than the last guy," Dom interjected. "He's never been arrested and is as clean as a whistle. He even used to be a bank executive."

I moved through the papers until I found our fourth and final Plymouth owner. His name was Charles Edward Duncan. There was very little information about him though. He was forty-nine years old and lived just across the river in the city of Hudson.

"Not much here," I commented.

"Like I said," Dom replied, "clean as a whistle."

Something bothered me. Dom had said that Duncan used to be a bank executive. That was not in the few papers I had seen.

"You said he used to be a bank executive?"

"Yeah," Dom said, taking another big gulp of coffee. "He was the head teller at the old Reliance Bank in Hudson."

Reliance Bank at one time was the biggest bank in Hudson. That was the better part of twenty years ago. Now it was out of business and remained one of many vacant buildings throughout upstate New York.

"I don't see anything about Duncan working at a bank in here," I offered. "How did you know that?"

Dom put his coffee cup down on my desk. He looked up and answered, "I used to have an account and I remember him. He was a nice guy and then one day, he was gone."

I started putting the papers back in the envelope. I was nearly done when Dom spoke again.

"The guy left his job after his wife died. It was a car accident."

Maybe it was because of recent events with Becky and my thoughts of guilt toward my late wife, but Dom's words hit me like a thunderbolt. I straightened up and nearly dropped the envelope. "What did you say about this guy's wife?" I asked.

Dom seemed startled by my sudden movement. He looked at me for a moment before replying. "She died in a car accident," he said. "I don't know anything else about it."

"Find out right away," I said. My tone seemed to confuse Dom. Before he could say anything, I held my hand up to silence him. "Just do it," I said again. "Call it another hunch."

Dom shrugged, pulled out his cell phone, and made a call. As he spoke with whoever answered, I reread all the documents, though in truth, my eyes were just scanning the words. My mind was racing. Hearing of the death of this guy's wife had triggered something. It could just be that I was hypersensitive given my own experiences.

My own life had been turned upside down after Melissa's death. I had even considered suicide on more than one occasion. Could such a thing also invoke homicidal ideation? It hadn't for me, though there had been times when I was filled with intense anger at the entire world. I had channeled my emotions into my job in New York City. I hid from my emotions and only allowed myself to cope with them slowly over a number of years. What if I hadn't had something to throw myself into? Would someone actually choose murder to release rage and inner torment? Though the idea sickened me, I couldn't reject the concept entirely.

I was still contemplating just how far pain and anger could push someone when Dom finished his call. "You may be onto something, pal," he said. "What happened to Duncan was more than just a car accident, and it wasn't just his wife who died."

I felt my stomach tighten as Dom continued speaking.

"I just talked to Hugh Thompson, the police chief over in Hudson. Old Hughie's a real great guy. We used to go fishing together over at Lake Taghkanic. One time, he caught this—"

"Dom," I said loudly, "stay focused. What about Duncan?"

"Oh yeah, sorry about that," Dom continued. "Hughie tells me that Duncan was driving with his wife and four-year-old daughter. A tractor trailer lost control, went over the center line, and hit Duncan's car at high speed. Duncan's wife and kid were killed instantly. He wasn't hit as bad and survived. He was taken to the hospital, but checked himself out after a few days. He left his job a week later."

As I absorbed this information, I tried to think of a question just so I could speak and not imagine the horror this guy had endured. Finally, I blurted out, "Where is he working now?"

"Hughie said he is emailing me everything he has on him. I should have it shortly."

I sat down in my chair. Neither of us said a word for several long minutes. I took a few more sips of my coffee. I was now convinced that Charles Edward Duncan was our killer. The information was nowhere near enough to convict him in a court of law. Yet, deep down where it really matters, I had no doubt whatsoever of his guilt. It is not a feeling easily explained. It was neither logical nor rational. It simply was.

A minute later, there was a shrill beeping sound. Dom checked his phone and announced that he had received the email. We took a few minutes to turn on my desk computer and log into Dom's email so I could view the documents while he saw them on his phone. Soon we had the email open. There were four attachments containing reports, photos, and other documents. We slowly went through them.

According to the police reports, it was a local business owner who made the initial call to the police. When they arrived at the scene, police found the tractor trailer lying on its side. After demolishing Duncan's car, it had flipped on the driver's side. The driver was dead on arrival.

Duncan's wife and kid were brutally mangled. The pictures of them were beyond disturbing and horrible. The little girl was unrecognizable. Her mother was belted into the front passenger seat. Her head was turned unnaturally far to the left, her neck obviously broken. Her face was covered in blood and frozen in a moment of fear. Her eyes were open and staring toward the driver's seat.

At first, police were unable to get Duncan out of the car. While they waited for the Jaws of Life to arrive, police photographers had obviously considered it a crime scene and taken a lot of pictures.

Perhaps the most disturbing picture was one taken of Charles Duncan himself. He was in the driver's seat. A small trickle of blood had run from above his hairline and had split when it reached his nose, causing two smaller lines of red on either side. His eyes were wide and his pupils looked fully dilated, like two black marbles. They had the appearance of shark's eyes, almost completely black and without even a glimmer of light or life. There was no emotion on his face. He was looking directly at his wife's lifeless remains.

The odd thing was that this man looked familiar to me. I had seen him before and recently. I just couldn't remember when or where.

There were also autopsy results for Duncan's wife and child, and records from Rockfield Medical Center. Despite the horrific crash, Charles Duncan had relatively few injuries. He was diagnosed with a few lacerations and bruises. The only significant laceration was one on the lower abdomen extending to the groin, which required quite a few stitches. There were recommendations of psychiatric follow-up, which was common after such a crash and terrible personal loss.

The police investigative reports showed that the truck driver had very high levels of alcohol in his blood, more than three times the legal limit. Not surprisingly, detectives determined that driver intoxication was the cause of the crash.

There were a few additional reports made by detectives who tried to speak with Charles Duncan after he left the hospital. They confirmed that he had quit his job at the bank. The last report, dated December 2, 1998, noted that Duncan had recently obtained a job as a delivery driver for a bakery doing overnight deliveries to delis and supermarkets.

This last note was only slightly less than three months before the murder of Kim Garrett, the first victim of the Rockfield Strangler.

I sat back in my chair, stunned at everything I had just read and seen. Everything fit my initial hunch. Duncan turned to murder after the horrific death of his wife and family. It seemed clear to me that he had been overwhelmed with grief, anger, and rage. It had driven him to violence and multiple murders.

What disturbed me even more was that I fully understood the anger and rage. I had felt it after Melissa's death, a senseless, mindless, and unrelenting fury at a God and a world that I perceived had allowed it to happen. I had never even considered murder, though I couldn't help but wonder if I could have. I had thought of taking my own life. Was I really that different from Charles Duncan? Were we actually two sides of the same coin?

"Connor?"

I looked up and saw Dom standing over me.

"You okay?" Dom asked, genuine concern on his face.

"I'm fine," I lied. Now was not the time for indecision. A killer needed to be stopped. My own doubts and self-recriminations would have to wait.

Dom didn't seem satisfied, but he let it go. "You think this is the guy?" he asked.

"No doubt."

"We have enough for a warrant?"

"Maybe," I said. "I'll have to get his exact address again for the papers. I just remember it is in Hudson."

"Yeah," Dom answered, "here's his most recent driver's license." He handed me his cell phone. I looked at it and saw Duncan's license. Instead of focusing on his address, I was drawn immediately to his photograph. His more recent appearance was very different. His dark hair was now parted on the right side. His eyes were not severely dilated and were a very bright shade of blue. I now remembered exactly when I had seen him.

"Holy shit," I said aloud.

"What is it?" Dom asked.

"That's the guy."

"What do you mean, Connor?"

"That son of a bitch was there!" I shouted. "He was sitting in the back of the courtroom when we dropped the charges against Clancy."

"Are you fucking shitting me?" Dom asked.

I ignored his question and said, "Now I have enough. Get together some detectives and evidence techs from Rockfield PD and meet me at Duncan's address in one hour."

Then I turned in my chair so I was facing the open door. "Casey," I shouted, "call Judge Hardy and tell him I will be in his chambers in thirty minutes with a search warrant for him to sign!"

20

Before writing up my warrant application, I instructed Casey to call the police department and have them move the reporters away from my office. I could not function if every time I opened the outside door, I was assailed by the press screaming questions.

Casey complied, though mumbled something while dialing about it being far easier to just shoot them.

The police arrived in a matter of minutes and soon the reporters were finally gone. Dom left with the police to organize our search party. I had to put together an application for a search warrant.

In less than thirty minutes, I was standing in Judge Hardy's chambers with my warrant application. I had added just about every factual allegation I had against Charles Duncan. I included his ownership of a 1973 Plymouth Scamp and attached pictures I had printed from the internet of both the 1973 Scamp and the Dodge Dart. I wanted to make sure the judge understood how easily these two cars could be confused. I topped it all off with an attorney's affirmation from me detailing my eyewitness account of the man in the courtroom and my subsequent realization that the man was Charles Duncan.

Hardy signed the warrant with very little comment and I took off for Hudson. I arrived at the home of Charles Duncan to find Dom waiting with a group of officers. Among them was Rockfield Police Chief of Detectives Adam Richards.

Richards was about my height but much heavier. He was easily over three hundred pounds and his belly sagged over his gun belt. His nose was red and bulbous, a classic drinker's nose. His love affair with Johnnie Walker Red was well known. In his prime, he had been an excellent detective, though in recent years both Scotch and his desire for retirement had taken over his life.

Richards saw me walking toward them and his still-strong voice bellowed over everyone else. "Hey, Mr. Special Prosecutor, can we get this fucking show on the road?" he yelled.

I ignored him and spoke directly to Dom Bryce. "Here's the warrant," I said, handing it to him. "What's our status?"

Before he could answer, Adam Richards tapped me on the shoulder. "Listen, hotshot," he snarled, "I'm the Chief of Detectives. These officers follow my orders. You got it?"

I stepped in front of his face, staring directly into his bloodshot eyes. I could smell the stale Scotch and cigarettes on his breath. "No, you listen, detective," I said in a soft, though intense tone, "I don't care if you're the king of the fucking world. This is my show and my operation. I call the shots. You're in charge of your officers, but the orders you give them come directly from me."

I paused for a second or two merely for effect and watched as the muscles under his paunch tensed up. Before he could even form a syllable, I spoke again. "You got it?" I asked.

Richards said nothing, but he was clearly enraged. His breath rattled in his lungs and throat more quickly, and I was almost surprised the aroma of Scotch and tobacco hadn't made me lose consciousness.

Dom quickly stepped between us and pushed both of us back. "We ain't got time for this bullshit," he said forcefully. He looked over to Richards and said, "You know he's in charge, Adam. Cut the shit."

The detective stood his ground for a moment and then turned away with a grunt.

I waited until I was satisfied that the confrontation was over. Then I asked Dom, "What is his problem?"

"Oh, don't mind him," Dom huffed. "He's still a decent cop. He may drink too much, but he's still honest and still pulls for the right team."

"Right team?" I asked.

"Cops," Bryce replied. "He's a cop all the way through. He doesn't trust you because most of the time you're a defense attorney."

"Yeah, yeah," I said, smirking, "a slimy defense mouthpiece."

Dom laughed before quickly turning to business. "We haven't entered the house yet," he said. "We've been waiting for the warrant. We did take a look around back. No sign of the car or Duncan. Our best guess is he's not home."

"Okay," I answered, "let's take a look around."

Dom walked to the front door and pounded loudly. "Mr. Duncan?" he yelled, "Rockfield Police Department. We have a warrant."

When there was no answer or any sign of movement, he signaled to several officers. Four of them came onto the front porch along with Detective Richards, who was carrying a portable battering ram.

Dom and the four officers drew their weapons and stood clear at each side of the door. Detective Richards moved forward. Whether it was the ram, Richard's weight, or both, the door flew open after only one strike. When it opened, Richards stepped back, allowing Dom and four officers to enter.

After a matter of minutes, the officers came out of the house. Dom came next and yelled, "Clear," signifying that the home was empty.

Dom and I, as well as two police technicians, pulled on coveralls, booties, hats, and gloves so as not to contaminate potential evidence. We also had to bring flashlights. Dom and his officers determined in their initial sweep that there was no power in the house. The service had apparently been turned off. In some of the rooms were old-fashioned kerosene or paraffin lamps with signs of recent use.

The four of us walked into the house and began to search.

The home was extremely tidy. It looked well maintained and perfectly normal, until we got to the second floor. There were three bedrooms and a bathroom. There was nothing unusual about the bathroom, though I did have one of the technicians collect a toothbrush and man's razor. I figured we could get some DNA from those items to compare to the known sample of the killer.

The first bedroom was like the rest of the home. The dressers were neatly packed with folded clothes and the one closet contained nothing of real importance.

The second and third bedrooms were both locked. I was about to force it open when one of the techs asked me to stand back. The door had an old-fashioned lock that opened with a metal skeleton key. The officer pulled out a ring of keys from his bag and tried them. On the third attempt, the lock clicked.

Inside was a room that looked like it had not been touched in years. There was a layer of dust on all surfaces. Before we even went inside, the very thorough police evidence team took video and snapped photos of the entire room. When they were finished, they let Dom and me take a look around.

It was a child's bedroom. There was a small bed on one side with an old wooden rocking chair nearby. The bed had a comforter on it with characters from *Sesame Street*. Lying on one of the pillows was a stuffed yellow duck. It was dirty and worn. It had obviously been a well-loved friend taken everywhere by its owner. On the other end of the room was a wooden box containing stuffed animals and toys. The dresser and closet contained clothes for a small girl.

The final bedroom had the identical type of lock and was quickly opened with the same key. We went through the same process of photographing and filming the entire room before searching it.

This room had clearly been the master bedroom at one time. Like the child's room, there was a layer of dust on everything. The closet and dresser on the far side of the bed contained a woman's clothes and shoes. The other closet and dresser were completely empty.

I instinctively understood what had happened. When his family died, Duncan had taken all of his stuff and moved into the third room. But rather than get rid of his family's belongings or even see them and be reminded, he had locked them away. Out of sight and out of mind. It was an idea that probably sounded good at the time, but I knew from experience that it was just a delay tactic.

When Melissa died, I initially wanted to keep everything she ever owned. Some part of me thought that if all of her possessions remained, then she wasn't really gone. Later, when that didn't work, I moved them all to the basement. I figured if I couldn't see them, they wouldn't bother me. I had been wrong.

Eventually, I was able to make the decision to get rid of some things, but keep those that really meant something. It had been difficult and very painful. It had helped, but was something I never wanted to do again. I guess it was a necessary pain and part of the process of saying goodbye.

From what I could see, Duncan never got to that point. He had locked everything away. He didn't want to let anything go, but couldn't bear to see them and feel that horrible pain I knew so well.

It reminded me once again how similar this killer was to me. We both faced devastating loss and tragedy, and had shut our lives down. We both endured terrible pain and loss. We both felt anger and hatred against the world. The only difference was that I ran away from my pain and lost myself to a job in New York City. Duncan turned his rage into murder. It bothered me that I had been so close to the road this killer had taken.

Robert Frost famously wrote about two divergent roads. He chose the one less traveled, claiming it made all the difference.

I wondered how he would describe the roads Duncan and I had each chosen.

I snapped back to reality when Dom called to me from the hallway. I stepped out and saw him pointing at a cord hanging from the ceiling. It was an entrance to an attic. I nodded and he pulled the cord, causing a wooden staircase to lower and extend.

I was about to send the evidence technicians up, but Dom waved them away. He pulled out his Colt 45 and started climbing the steps before disappearing from sight. I realized that during the initial search, they must have missed the attic. Now he had to make sure that Duncan wasn't hiding up there.

A minute later, I heard Dom exclaim, "Holy shit!"

Thinking he was in trouble, I moved as quickly as I could to the ladder and started climbing. I was almost to the point where I could see into the attic when Dom reappeared at the very top. The look on his face told me without a word that he had found something both important and horrible.

"Connor," he said, signaling me to stop, "send the evidence boys up here first."

"What's up there, boss?" I asked urgently.

Dom shook his head. "You have to see it. Just send the boys up to take photos and video. Then you can see it."

I wanted to burst past him and see for myself, but I knew that if I did, I could compromise the evidentiary value of whatever was up there, so I went back down the ladder and the two officers went up with their cameras.

Though it was probably only ten minutes or so of waiting, it felt much longer. I was nervously pacing back and forth as I speculated at what Dom had found. Was it another body? Was it something even worse?

After what seemed like an eternity, Dom yelled to me that it was okay for me to come up. I climbed the ladder quickly and entered the attic.

It was partially finished with wooden planks laid across the joists. On either side of the attic, there was a space of about three or four feet without boards. The entire attic was empty except for the very center, where some old tables of varying heights had been pushed together to form a tabletop surface of between fifteen and eighteen feet across. There was a pile of items on each. Dom and the two officers were standing in front of them.

I walked over and Dom pointed at the first table, a metal bridge table. There was a pile of clothes and a pair of tennis shoes on it. The clothes consisted of black jeans, a pink shirt, and white bra and panties. The panties were stained red with blood. On the shirt was a name tag that read, "Kimmy." Inside the shoes were white socks speckled with blood. Next to the clothes was a woman's purse. Inside was a wallet. The driver's license in the wallet revealed that the purse belonged to Kim Garrett, the first victim of the Strangler.

On the other side of the clothes were newspaper clippings

that detailed the discovery of Garrett's body and the media coverage.

The next two nearly identical tables had bloody clothing and personal items belonging to Darlene Johnson and Susanna Hoskins. There were also newspaper clippings about their cases.

The fourth was a dented metal folding table with two legs previously repaired with duct tape. It had newspaper clippings and a black composition pad with a white label. Written in red on the label in big block letters was "AMY ALLEN." I picked up the notebook and opened it. Inside were notes written in red ink. The first page was dated June 18, 2000. The note was brief but ominous.

Two people interrupted before release. Choke not complete. Girl not dead. Had to run away.

Newspaper says girl named Amy Allen. She described me. Can identify me. Must complete. Pain getting worse. Have to release.

The next page was dated June 28, 2000. It read:

Saw her last night sitting on porch

was almost there

cops!! A trap. Run

AMY ALLEN IS TALISMAN. EVIL. CANNOT KILL.

The last written page was dated February 7, 2015. Taped to the page was the obituary of Amy Allen. In large block letters below, Duncan had written, "TALISMAN DEAD. I AM FREE."

The fifth was a plastic folding table that would normally be used for outdoor events. It was white, but stained from age and use. I was not surprised to find the clothes and personal effects of Michelle Coleman piled on top. There were also newspaper clippings about the murder and later arrest of Bob Clancy.

The very next table seemed out of place. It had large piles of matted fur and dried blood. I had no idea what types of fur I was seeing, but some looked like they could have been from cats and dogs. There were a few larger pieces as well. Off to the side of the furs were dark twisted things that looked like they were made of hardened rubber. I took a close look and felt my stomach twitch as I realized they were likely internal organs that had once been inside those furs.

I looked over to Dom to see if he had any explanation for this display. One look from him made it clear that he was just as mystified as I was. I decided to move on.

What I had seen thus far was disturbing and horrifying. Yet, what I saw on the final table caused my breath to catch in my throat and my blood to run cold. The table was new and painted white. On it, at the very top, was a complete newspaper. It was this morning's edition announcing the return of the Rockfield Strangler.

Directly below the newspaper were words written on the surface of the table with a bright red Sharpie. It read:

I WILL RELEASE FOREVER MY PAIN
AS I HEAR YOUR LAST BREATH
RIP
CONNOR PHELAN

21

The technicians were busy collecting the mountain of evidence from Duncan's attic. Dom and I had made our way out of the house, and stripped off our coveralls, booties, and gloves. Now we were standing by my Cherokee, trying to comprehend everything we had just seen.

"That's one crazy motherfucker," Dom said, breaking the silence as only he could.

I laughed at the absurdity of it all. "Can't argue with that," I answered.

We stood staring at each other for a minute before Dom spoke again. "Hey, pal," he said, "can you give me a lift back to your office? The guys picked me up there and brought me here, so I don't have my car."

"Sure," I said, "hop in."

We got in the car and started driving. We were only a few minutes into the trip when Dom broached the only subject we were thinking about: Charles Edward Duncan.

"None of this makes sense to me. I understand that he lost his mind when his family died," Dom said, "but why is he coming after you? And what is this *talisman* shit?"

These were the same questions my mind had been focusing on from the moment I read the threat written in blood-red ink. I had a theory. It wasn't great, but it was the best I had.

"I think it started with Amy Allen," I replied. "She survived his attack. He tried to kill her again and his notes suggest the police showed up. He seems to think it was a setup. I guess he thought Amy Allen was some kind of hex against him—that her living was somehow a curse against him."

"That makes no fucking sense," Dom interrupted. "A talisman's a good luck charm."

"I know that," I agreed, "but you can't expect a deranged mind to think logically."

Dom laughed. "So, why is he after you?" he asked. "And what is this 'release forever my pain' shit?"

"No idea about that, boss," I said as I turned onto Oak Street, "but he's probably coming for me because of that damn newspaper."

"That makes sense, I guess." Dom paused for a moment before asking, "How did the paper find out about the DNA? I thought you were keeping that under wraps."

"I was," I replied angrily. "It had to be Worthington who leaked it. That son of a bitch tried to hurt my investigation so I would fail. Then he could take over and be the fucking hero."

Dom shifted in his seat when he heard this. "That no-good lying fuck," he groused. "I ought to knock him flat on his arrogant ass."

"Leave him to me. I'll deal with it."

Dom knew from my tone that it was best not to talk further about Worthington, so he steered the conversation back to our suspect. "Duncan knows we have his DNA. What I don't get is why he thinks killing you will get rid of the DNA," he said.

"Like I said, he's a few clowns short of a circus," I responded, causing both of us to burst into laughter.

Dom was still laughing when I saw it. Right ahead, in the parking lot of my law office was the gray 1973 Plymouth Scamp. Duncan was likely in my office. If he was, Casey was in real danger, if she wasn't dead already.

I jammed on the brakes and stopped in the middle of the street. Dom nearly flew into the dashboard. "Hey, what the fuck?" he shouted, trying to regain his seat.

I pointed at the Plymouth in the parking lot. Dom saw it and a look of fear crossed his face.

"Casey!" Dom screamed, pulling out his Colt. He threw open his door, jumped out of the car, and ran toward the front door.

I was surprised at how quickly he had moved. I pulled the car over, parked, and followed him. By the time I got to the front door, Dom had already burst through and I could hear screaming inside. I entered and initially saw Dom pointing his gun and yelling, "Let her go, scumbag!"

On the other side of the room was Charles Edward Duncan. He had Casey in a choke lock. His right arm was around her throat and he was squeezing as hard as he could. Her eyes were closed and she looked unconscious.

"I'll kill the bitch," Duncan growled, his voice menacing and beyond intimidating. "Drop your gun."

"I said let her go, you piece of shit!" Dom yelled again.

Duncan's eyes were wild. His pupils were dilated and had the same shark-like appearance from the accident photos. The rest of his face was contorted in rage.

Casey was not moving. I knew that if she had been choked unconscious, she only had a matter of minutes before she died, and I had no idea how long the choke had been applied. Dom could not shoot and risk hitting Casey, but I had nothing stopping me.

I pushed past Dom and lunged at Duncan. I grabbed his right arm with both hands and pulled, trying to break his grip.

As we struggled, our eyes locked. One of the things I had always been good at when questioning witnesses was being able to read their eyes. But when I looked into Duncan's eyes, there was nothing there. His face showed rage, but his eyes were cold and devoid of emotion or life.

His arm was starting to loosen when he suddenly screamed in fury. As he did, he pushed Casey right at me. I lost my balance and fell backward with Casey right onto Dom. The three of us went to the floor with Casey landing on top of me.

I rolled to my left side, causing Casey to slide off me and to the floor. By the time I got to my feet, Duncan was already out the back door. I took a quick look back and saw Dom checking on Casey. Knowing she was in good hands, I ran out of the back door after Duncan.

When I had taken a few steps into the parking lot, I saw Duncan about twenty-five feet ahead of me. He was near his car, facing me with his right hand held back by his head, like he was about to throw a baseball. I saw a glint of metal in his hand as it came forward, and instinctively dove to my left. The hunting knife Duncan had thrown stuck into the wooden doorframe, and I crashed into a large plastic recycling bin before slamming down hard on the concrete.

I again struggled to my feet. As I did, I heard a car door close and then an engine roared to life. I started forward as Duncan put the car into gear and began backing out of the lot. I ran toward him and jumped onto the hood of the car. He accelerated out of the parking lot with me clinging to one of the windshield wipers, realizing I had just done something very stupid.

He turned the wheel and the car spun onto the main road with the tires screeching loudly. I did my best to hang on, but the momentum was simply too much. The wiper snapped off, and I slid off the hood and was airborne. I collided with the side of a parked car and fell to the road. I tried to stand. I couldn't.

My head was pounding and the nausea was overwhelming. As I lay there, I heard Duncan's car drive away.

Although I didn't feel like it, I realized that I had been very lucky. Jumping on his car had been very foolish. I was fortunate I hadn't been killed. If the fall hadn't done the job, Duncan could have stopped and come right after me. I was so dizzy, I wasn't sure any amount of judo would have saved me. I decided, as I pulled myself to my feet about a minute later, that stupid things like that were best left to 1980s television shows.

I took only a few steps before another wave of nausea caused me to fall to my knees. I tilted my head back and took a few deep breaths. I knew I had again aggravated my concussion. I also knew that Casey had been choked at least unconscious and was possibly dead.

I willed myself to my feet and stumbled down the street toward my office. I could hear sirens getting closer. I assumed Dom had called for an ambulance. I finally reached the front door and entered. As I did, I heard someone talking. I quickly realized that the one talking was Dom. I thought hopefully that Casey had woken up and was talking.

I took a few steps forward and realized I was wrong. Dom was sitting on the floor next to Casey. She was lying on her back, her eyes closed. I could see by the movement of her chest that she was breathing.

What really surprised me was Dom. He had always been a tough-as-nails retired cop who never showed any emotion other than being pissed off. Yet, as he gently stroked Casey's cheek, tears were running down his face. "Come on, kid, stay with me," he said, his voice choked with emotion. "You always say how tough you are. Prove it."

Casey made no movement.

I froze. I wanted to rush in and check on Casey. Yet, I felt somehow that doing so would be intruding on something.

Dom and Casey were always needling each other. Anyone watching them for five minutes would assume they hated each other. I knew better. I remembered a time about a year ago when Dom and I got into an argument. I had complained to Casey about him and was shocked when she defended him. "Oh, he's not so bad," she had said. "He's like that crazy uncle everyone has."

Now as I watched Dom, I began to realize how he really saw her. Dom had two ex-wives, but had never had children with either. He always made some excuse about kids being a pain in the ass. As he knelt over Casey and cried, I somehow understood that Casey was the daughter he never had.

I heard some commotion behind me. Two paramedics came through the door with a gurney. I stepped aside and let them pass. Dom heard them too. He stood and quickly wiped his eyes with his sleeve, clearly hoping nobody had noticed. He then spoke with the paramedics, telling them what had occurred.

When Dom saw me, he walked quietly over. We both stood there in silence as the men worked over her. They put a medical collar on Casey's neck and started strapping her to a spinal board. Given that she had been assaulted and viciously choked, they were concerned that she might have a broken neck.

The look on Dom's face still showed grief, but it was quickly replaced by anger. "That mutt get away?" he asked coldly.

"Yeah," I mumbled, "he's gone."

"He's gonna pay for this," Dom vowed. "I'll find him and I'll kill him."

I put my hand on his shoulder as the paramedics finished getting Casey on the gurney and started wheeling her out.

"Take it easy, old buddy," I said, "we'll catch him."

We followed them out the door and watched in silence as they lifted the gurney with Casey and slid it into the back of the ambulance.

"Dom, you go with her," I urged. "I'll call her family and supervise the collection of evidence from here."

"You will do no such thing," a whiny voice suddenly announced.

I whirled around and saw DA Worthington standing nearby.

"The assault against Miss Franklin is a new and separate case and my office will handle it," he announced arrogantly.

I wondered how he could possibly have known what had happened. It had only been a matter of minutes since we walked in on Duncan choking Casey. I quickly realized what must have happened. Worthington must have been listening to the county 911 scanner and heard Dom's call for an ambulance. I assumed he must have mentioned on the call that Casey had been assaulted. When he heard what had happened, Worthington scurried right over from the courthouse.

It was bad enough that this jerk was trying once again to interject himself into my case. What really had me steamed was that there was no doubt that he had been the one to tip off the newspaper that the recent murder marked the return of the Rockfield Strangler. I had been worried that making things public would cause the killer to go into hiding. Instead, it had caused him to target me. He came to my office looking to kill me, and when I wasn't there, he went after Casey.

Dom must have been thinking the same thing because before I could even respond, he rushed past me and yelled, "You filthy cocksucker, this is your fault!"

Worthington opened his mouth, but never got the chance to utter a word. Dom punched him right in the face, knocking the district attorney on his back. Worthington looked up from the concrete. His nose was gushing blood and was clearly broken.

Dom was not satisfied. He reached down and grabbed Worthington by the collar, causing the bleeding man to whimper in pain and fright.

I grabbed Dom from behind and pulled him back. He released Worthington's collar, but fought violently to get out of my grip. It was all I could do to hold him.

"This is not going to help Casey!" I yelled. "Neither is decking that asshole."

"The motherfucker deserved it!" he shouted back. Realizing he could not get loose, he stopped fighting me. Hoping he would not just charge and attack, I released him. As I let him go, Dom pointed an accusing finger down at Worthington. "You leaked the DNA report to the newspaper and that's why Casey got hurt."

"I don't know what you're talking about," Worthington sniveled, his voice now worse as the blood from his broken nose continued to flow. "I didn't—"

"Save your bullshit!" I shouted back. "We know damn well that you did."

"That's a lie," Worthington answered back, now starting to choke and cough from the blood. "Both of you are going to jail."

I stepped away from Dom and knelt right in front of the district attorney. He put his hands and arms over his face in a pathetic attempt at self-defense.

"I'm not going to hit you," I said, "though I want to."

Worthington lowered his arms slowly, not quite sure he believed me.

I pointed my finger at him just like Dom had moments ago. "You listen to me and you listen good," I said threateningly. "We know you leaked it and, more important, Judge Hardy knows it."

"So what if I did?" he finally admitted. He started to speak again, but I cut him right off.

"Don't say another word or I'll let Dom finish what he started," I said as Worthington's eyes went wide with terror. "You thought you'd fuck up my investigation and make me look bad.

What you actually did was tip off the killer, and he came to my office and attacked my office manager."

I was becoming more and more angry as I spoke. This caused the volume of my voice and the pain in my head to increase dramatically. I stood back up and took a quick breath to maintain my composure before continuing.

"Dom," I said, as he turned to look at me, "get in the ambulance and go with Casey to the hospital. I'll be there shortly."

Dom looked back at Worthington and glared angrily. Then he strode over to the ambulance and climbed through the rear door. When the ambulance pulled away, I turned back to Worthington, who was now sitting on the ground.

"I was going to put together every shred of proof I have and send it to the ethics committee, so they could investigate and possibly suspend your law license," I said, "but somehow, Dom's solution seems a little more appropriate."

As I was speaking, two police cars drove up with lights and sirens. They stopped and four young patrolmen came bursting out.

I walked away from Worthington and toward the officers. "Gentlemen," I said, "I'm Special Prosecutor Phelan. Please come with me."

The men immediately followed. Just as we reached the door to my office, one of the officers spoke. "Excuse me, sir," he asked, "but what about District Attorney Worthington?"

I looked back. Worthington was starting to get to his feet. He had a handkerchief in his hand and was holding it to his nose. He was still coughing and sputtering. I despised the prick and felt he got what he deserved. Yet, I couldn't just let him bleed in the street. *Damn conscience,* I thought.

I looked at the officer who asked the question. His nameplate identified him as Officer Collins.

"Collins, check on Mr. Worthington," I said. "Call for another ambulance if he needs it."

The young patrolman quickly jogged over to Worthington. As he did, I looked at the other officers and said, "You three are with me," before leading them into my office.

22

Shortly after we entered the office, Police Chief Jim Taylor made an appearance. Jim had been chief for nearly thirty years. He was hard-nosed and no-nonsense. He was both respected and feared by his men, though he was also well known for backing officers loyal to him. He was a man used to handling things his own way.

When Taylor walked in, all three patrolmen stopped what they were doing and stood at attention. The chief ignored them and walked right up to me. "You mind telling me what's going on here and what in the name of Jesus H. Christ happened to Rob Worthington?" he demanded in a voice barely above a whisper, but with all the seriousness of a heart attack. "I just ordered Collins to take him down to the ER to get his crooked beak fixed."

I didn't want to answer his question in front of so many witnesses. I pointed to my inner office and said, "Can we talk privately?"

Once we were inside, I closed the door. Taylor sat down in one of the guest chairs. He reached into his pocket and pulled out a brown wooden billiard pipe. He put it in his mouth before reaching into another pocket and retrieving a lighter. Without a word or even asking for permission, Taylor lit his pipe and took a few deep puffs. Then, apparently satisfied with the taste and smell of the smoke, he looked up at me and waited patiently for me to speak.

I wasn't at all happy that he was smoking in my office. Given the circumstances, however, I felt it best not to object. Truth be told, I was impressed with how he had taken full control of our discussion without saying a word. It was a technique I would definitely have to learn.

I got right to the point and told him how Worthington had leaked the DNA evidence to the newspaper, and how the killer had targeted me in response, but attacked Casey when he didn't find me. Finally, I told him how Dom blamed Worthington for Casey getting hurt and shattered his nose.

Throughout the explanation, Chief Taylor said nothing, though he gave a very slight smile when I described Dom's punch. He inhaled from the pipe deeply, held it for a moment, and then released the smoke ever so slowly. Then he leaned forward to speak. "You're sure it was Worthington who leaked to the paper?" he asked.

"He admitted it," I replied.

Jim looked off slightly to his right as he considered my words. Then he made eye contact with me again. "Sounds to me like the prick got what he deserved. But now there's the issue of criminal charges, isn't there?"

This thought had already occurred to me. Though Dom was the one who actually threw the punch, Worthington would look to nail both of us. I could expect him to claim a conspiracy of some kind. He wouldn't stop there. Worthington would probably file a complaint against me with the professional conduct committee in Albany. Ultimately, I wouldn't lose my license, but there would be a lengthy inquiry. It would be a genuine pain in the ass. Worthington would revel in it. I almost wanted to deck him myself.

"Look, chief, I—"

"I'll make sure there aren't any charges," he interrupted. "The DA won't take any action against you or Dom." He then resumed inhaling from his pipe.

I was stunned to say the least. Granted, Taylor was the police chief, but Worthington was the district attorney. It was his decision who got charged and who didn't.

"I appreciate that, chief," I offered, "but how in the hell are you going to—"

"Don't worry about how," Taylor said firmly, "I'll get it done."

I decided to let the matter drop. There was something about the chief's calm demeanor and confident tone that made me realize he could do exactly as he had said. I reasoned that Jim Taylor must have something on Worthington. Almost nothing else would stop a weasel like him. I wondered what secret the chief had on the district attorney, but quickly determined it was better if I didn't know.

"Thanks, chief," I finally said, "I guess I owe you one."

Chief Taylor's eyes widened. He took the pipe out of his mouth, smiled, and said, "You certainly do, counselor."

The look on Jim Taylor's face told me beyond a shadow of a doubt that he would one day come calling to collect this debt. When he did, it would be something big. Somehow, I also knew that he wasn't going to ask anything of me right away. He was going to hold it in his pocket until the opportune moment. I wasn't thrilled to owe anyone such a big favor, but had little choice.

Without another word, Taylor stood. He shouted for one of his officers. The young recruit nearly flew through the door. "Yes, sir?" he asked nervously.

Taylor stepped right up to the patrolman and looked him in

the eyes. "Listen to me carefully, Officer Wilkins, and do exactly as I say. No more and no less. You got it?"

"Yes, sir," Wilkins replied obediently.

"Get on the horn and get an evidence tech over here on the double. I want this office checked for physical evidence. Understood?"

"Yes, sir," Wilkins answered, moving ever so slightly toward the door.

"And then," Taylor said, raising his voice slightly and causing Wilkins to stiffen back to attention, "get your keister over to Rockfield Medical Center. I want an officer standing guard outside Casey Franklin's hospital room."

This time, Wilkins did not move one iota in case there were more instructions. After a few seconds, Chief Taylor barked, "Go!" Wilkins nearly collided with the door on his way out.

When he was gone, Taylor took yet another drag on his pipe. He exhaled the smoke and turned back to me. "You going to the hospital too?" he asked.

I wanted to go right away, but didn't want to make a clumsy exit like Taylor's scared minion. I also realized that I owed Taylor a second favor. In the heat of the moment, I had not taken the time to realize that Duncan might try to finish the job and kill Casey.

I tried to offer my thanks, but when I opened my mouth, the words choked in my throat. My emotions were raw and barely under control. I was scared and worried for Casey. I knew she was unconscious when the paramedics took her. For all I knew, she might be dead. I was also angry at myself. The Strangler came looking for me, but Casey got hurt.

I suddenly remembered the dented metal folding table in Duncan's attic. The words from the black notebook on that table came back to me instantly.

...interrupted before release. Choke not complete. Girl not dead.

She described me. Can identify me. Must complete. Pain getting worse. Have to release.

I didn't fully understand the ravings of this deranged killer. What I did understand was that Dom and I had interrupted Duncan before he was finished. The last time this happened was when he tried to kill Amy Allen. According to his notebook, Duncan had gone back and tried to kill her right away.

I could not allow this to go any further. I vowed that I would find Duncan and stop him once and for all. I also decided then and there that if Casey died, there would be no trial. I would kill Duncan with my bare hands.

Taylor's voice broke through my thoughts. "Phelan?" he asked. "You okay?"

"Yeah, chief," I said. "Just lost in thought for a moment."

Taylor must have understood. He took the pipe out of his mouth and simply said, "Go. I'll handle things here. Check on your secretary. You have my word that we will just collect evidence. We won't look at any of your files."

I still did not have words, so I extended my hand and he shook it. I then hurried out of my office.

The drive to the hospital could not have taken more than ten minutes, but it seemed to last forever. As I drove, more visions flashed through my mind of those tables in Duncan's attic. I saw again the piles of clothing and the bloody animal furs. I saw the bright red letters on the last table. "RIP CONNOR PHELAN." I could feel anger burning within my chest and extending through my arms.

When I finally got to the hospital, I barely noticed where I left the Cherokee. I slammed it into park and was out the door. I almost ran into one of the nurses coming off shift as I went through the ER door. She gave me a dirty look, and I apologized as I went by.

I got to the admission desk, but there was nobody there. I

saw a metal call bell. I started ringing it over and over. When the bell rang for about the eleventh time, a hand slammed down on my finger, abruptly silencing it.

I looked up and saw a nurse standing there. Her identification tag revealed her name to be Hammonds. Nurse Hammonds was probably only five foot three, but she had a presence about her that would make even the bravest man hesitate. She was a woman who clearly took no shit from anyone. The look on her face made it clear that she was less than pleased with me. "One ring is sufficient, sir," she scolded in an authoritarian tone. "Can I help you?"

I quickly apologized, explained who I was, and asked for Casey Franklin. The nurse looked at me for a moment and said, "You sure you don't need treatment?"

I was confused for a second, but then remembered my swollen eye. I smiled and instinctively reached up to touch it. My finger came back with blood on it. My ride on the hood of Duncan's car and the crash landing thereafter must have reopened one of my cuts. There was only a little blood, so I ignored it. "I'm fine, nurse. Thank you," I said, "What I really need is to see Casey Franklin. She was attacked at my office."

Hammonds said nothing for a moment. Then she opened a drawer in her desk and pulled out something wrapped in paper. She handed it to me and turned to her computer.

In my hand was a wrapped gauze pad. As Hammonds tapped a few keys, I tore open the packet, pulled out the white pad, and gently placed it against my eye.

A moment later, Hammonds gruffly said, "Go to the double doors. I'll buzz you in."

I walked to the doors and the buzzer sounded just as I got there. I pushed them open and walked in. Beyond, I could see the nurses' station ahead on the left and a series of curtains on the right marking the trauma rooms.

Hammonds bellowed from the admission desk, "She's in trauma room three. Number's on the curtain."

I thanked her and walked quickly down the hall toward number three. Officer Wilkins was there, standing guard. He must have really moved once he got his orders. He nodded to me as I walked past him. The curtain to the trauma room was pulled back. I saw Dom first. He was sitting in a chair at the left end of the hospital bed. I could see only the very end of the bed. Dom looked over to me. He said nothing, but signaled me forward. I took a few more steps, not knowing exactly what I would see.

When the entire hospital bed came into view, I saw Casey. She was sitting up. Her eyes were open. She turned her head slowly to me. Her neck had an ugly bruise on the left side. When she saw me, she got that usual frustrated look. She smirked and spoke. Her voice was gravelly and sounded almost painful. "I better get that fucking raise now."

Dom burst out laughing. Casey's voice was strained, but her personality was as strong as ever. I thought what she said was beyond funny, but as I started to laugh, I suddenly felt tears running down my face. I had been feeling a whirlwind of emotion for the past few hours. It had started with almost elation when I got the search warrant. It had then changed to horror at the discovery of what was in Duncan's attic and fluctuated between fear, anger, rage, and shock from when we encountered Duncan in my office right through my drive to the hospital. When I saw and heard Casey, I briefly felt elation.

However, it was none of these emotions or even the combination of them causing my tears. The one emotion flooding over me and stifling all others was guilt. Everything that had occurred was my fault. I could blame Worthington for leaking information to the media. I could certainly blame Charles Edward Duncan. He had been the one who attacked her. Dom had already dealt with Worthington. However, his broken nose was nothing compared to what I wanted to do to Duncan.

My anger was still there, but it was overwhelmed by guilt. What I really felt deep down in my core was that Casey had been attacked and was in that hospital bed because of me. There was no other reason. Duncan chose her because of me. He had come for me and found only her. I was the one he wanted to kill and hurt. Casey was just collateral damage.

Casey just stared at me, her eyes starting to glisten. Without another word, I walked over to the side of the bed and sat down. I leaned in and hugged her.

"I'm sorry, kid," I said, trying to get my emotions back in check.

"Who are you calling kid?" she answered immediately.

I laughed slightly and started to pull away. I hadn't got even an inch when she tightened her grip and pulled me in. Then she began to cry.

23

It wasn't long before tears were replaced by stubbornness. Dom and I sat with Casey for nearly three hours. During this time, nurses came in periodically. Whenever any of us asked for an update, we were told that the doctor was reviewing the X-rays and test results. He would be in shortly.

The doctor finally arrived at almost half past four. He was well into his seventies and what little hair he had was as white as snow. He glanced down at the medical chart through glasses at the end of his nose. Then he looked up and announced that he was transferring Casey to a private room for the night.

Casey insisted she was fine and wanted to go home. The doctor tried in vain to convince his patient. They argued for several minutes before the old doctor finally gave up and left.

Dom and I tried to convince Casey it was best for her to stay in the hospital overnight for observation, but she was having none of it. It seemed like a hopeless cause until Casey's mother came flying into the emergency room. I always thought my office manager was headstrong. Her mother, Virginia Franklin, was more than that. She was a human hurricane.

She was about the same size as her daughter, but that was

the only physical similarity. Whereas Casey had long dark brown hair and wore bright vibrant colors (usually with cleavage showing), Virginia's hair was gray and closely cropped. She wore cream-colored pants and a matching turtleneck sweater. Her face was mostly hidden between large round glasses that gave her an owlish appearance.

Their personalities, however, strongly resembled one another. They were both strong-willed, though the elder Franklin was still the top banana, especially with Casey's voice still weak.

"What's this I hear about you going home, young lady?" Virginia roared.

"I'm fine, Mom," Casey croaked back, her voice weakening by the second. "I just want to go home and—"

"Nonsense," Virginia interrupted, wagging her finger. "Listen to your voice. You sound like you're gargling razorblades."

"Other than my voice, there's nothing wrong with me," Casey protested.

"For heaven's sake, your doctor says you were attacked and nearly choked to death," Virginia insisted. "I've told you a thousand times that you need to take better care of yourself. Instead, you just want to ignore your doctor. What if you have a concussion? What if you have internal injuries? You need to listen to what I..."

As Casey's mother kept talking, the pace of her voice got faster and faster, almost as if someone had pressed a fast-forward button.

I started backing away. It was apparent to me that Casey was not going to win this battle. She couldn't even get a word in edgewise. I was getting out of Dodge before the windbag turned her ire on me. Dom seemed to have the same idea because he was already out of the trauma room and headed for the exit.

Casey glanced over to me with a look that screamed, "Help

me!" I just shrugged my shoulders and mouthed the words, "Good luck" before heading down the hallway after Dom. I could still hear Casey's mother talking nonstop all the way down the hall and through the double doors. Dom was waiting for me on the other side.

"Wow, I thought Casey was a chatterbox," Dom finally said. "Her mother's mouth moves like a whippoorwill's ass."

"At least now we know where she gets it from," I offered.

While we were still laughing, my phone rang. I looked at the screen and saw it was Becky. I slid my finger across the screen and answered. I barely got the word "hello" out of my mouth before Becky jumped right in.

"Oh my God, Connor," she shouted, "I just heard the news on TV! I'm so sorry about Casey. I know how fond of her you were."

"Were?" I asked. "Why are you talking in the past tense?"

"She's alive?"

"Yes," I answered incredulously. "She was choked unconscious, but she's going to be fine. Why did you think she was dead?"

"The TV news reported that the Strangler killed a woman who worked in your office," Becky said defensively. "If it wasn't Casey, then who was it?"

"Nobody." I tried to keep my growing frustration out of my voice. "He attacked Casey, but Dom and I stopped him before he killed her. Unfortunately, he got away."

"So, everyone's okay?"

"Yeah, Casey's being held overnight for observation and I slightly reopened the cut on my eye and aggravated my concussion," I said before adding, "I'm fine though."

"The Strangler hit you?" Becky asked.

"No, it happened after I jumped on a moving car," I said, regretting my words immediately.

"You did what?!" Becky screamed. "Why the hell did you—"

"It's a long story."

"And one I want to hear."

"Look, I'll tell you all about it," I offered, seeing a chance to change the subject, "but now I need to eat. I worked right through lunch and I'm starving. You free to join me?"

"Sure," she replied, "I'm off tonight. Where do you want to go?"

"Do you know a place called The Cardinal?"

"You mean Eddie's place?" she asked.

"That's the one."

"I haven't been there in a long time," Becky said, "but it would be nice to see Eddie again. I can meet you there in about thirty minutes. Okay?"

"Sounds great," I said. "See you there."

I disconnected the call and turned to Dom. "I'm meeting Becky for dinner. You care to join us?"

Dom shook his head. "No, I don't want to be the third wheel."

I opened my mouth to respond, but Dom held up his hand to stop me. "Besides, I plan on staying here in case that scumbag comes back."

I told him about the news broadcast that Becky had heard. "If she is being reported as dead, why would Duncan come back?" I asked.

"No," Dom said defiantly, "I'm not going to assume he saw that. If he thinks she's alive, he will come back. You saw that shit in his fucking attic. I'm not going to let him get anywhere near Casey again, you got that?" Dom's voice cracked slightly with emotion as he finished his sentence. I knew there was no way I was going to convince him to leave the hospital. I'd seen his tears at my office when he thought Casey might not pull through, and I heard his emotion just now. I decided to let it go.

"Okay," I finally answered, "I'll stop by later. You want me to bring you anything? Maybe some of the shitty fish pizza?"

Dom snorted a stifled laugh. "No, I'll just get something from the hospital cafeteria."

"Yeesh," I said, as I turned for the exit, "I'd rather eat the shitty pizza."

I went straight to my Cherokee and headed off to The Cardinal. On the way, I thought about everything that had happened over the past few hours. I was grateful that Casey was still alive. I smiled as I thought that if she could handle her mother's verbal barrage, then surviving the Rockfield Strangler was a piece of cake.

Within twenty minutes after my phone call with Becky, I walked into The Cardinal. Eddie was behind the bar, his usual apron tied around his waist and a nearly empty glass of beer in his hand. As soon as he saw me, he did something he rarely did. He put down his beer. He came out from behind the bar and grabbed me by both shoulders. "I heard what happened, Clubber," he said with genuine concern in his voice. "Is everybody okay?"

"Yeah, boss, everyone's fine," I answered. "I guess you heard the false news about Casey being killed?"

"Yeah, I heard," he said, letting go of my shoulders. "They did a second report admitting they fucked up and that nobody was killed. People were just hurt. Just hurt? Can you believe that shit? Insensitive assholes."

I was actually relieved. Dom had been right to stay at the hospital. With this new report, there was a real chance that Duncan would try to finish what he started.

I quickly brought Eddie up to date. He swore when I described seeing Duncan choking Casey. When I finished, Eddie visibly relaxed.

"You should've killed the fucker, Clubber," he said before going behind the bar.

I sat on one of the barstools to continue our conversation. As I did, Eddie pulled a bottle of Glendalough from underneath the counter.

"Not tonight, boss," I said, "I'm meeting someone."

Eddie's eyes lit up. "You got a date?"

"It's not exactly a date," I said quickly.

"Are you meeting a woman?"

"Yes."

"Is this a woman you're interested in?"

"Well, yes."

"Is this woman attractive?"

"What is this? Cross examination?" I asked accusingly.

"The witness will answer the question," Eddie barked in his best judge voice.

"Objection," I said in reply.

"Objection denied. My bar. My court. My rules," Eddie insisted.

I rolled my eyes in frustration, but decided to just get it over with. "Fine," I said. "Yes, she's attractive."

"Then it's a date," Eddie announced with a look of smug satisfaction on his face.

I threw my hands up in mock surrender. "Call it whatever you want."

"Anything happen yet?"

"You know I never talk about shit like that."

"You fucked her," Eddie announced, causing the few other patrons in the place to look over in annoyance.

"Holy shit, dude," I replied, "keep your fucking voice down."

"Don't lie to me, man," Eddie pressed, his voice mercifully lower.

"Let's just say... we've become more than just friends and leave it at that," I said quietly.

Eddie leaned over the bar and whispered to me, "That means you fucked her," before smiling and pulling back to his side of the counter.

"I am not confirming that," I said.

"And you ain't denying it either."

I did not bother replying.

After a few seconds, Eddie decided to speak again. "So, who is she? Do I know her?"

I knew as soon as I told him, he was going to go wild again. It was better, though, to have it happen now than when Becky arrived. I looked away from Eddie to avoid eye contact and said, "Becky Foster."

His reaction was not at all what I expected.

"Well, it's about time," he said. "You were always pining over her in school. Over twenty years later, it finally happened. Good for you."

I was very uncomfortable talking about this subject. The whole thing was still very new to me and I had not reconciled my feelings about it. Whenever I was with Becky, everything felt right. When I was not, I felt guilty as if I was somehow being unfaithful to my wife.

Eddie must have read the look on my face. He slammed his fist down on the bar. "You gotta be fucking kidding me!"

"What now?" I asked in exasperation.

"You're thinking of calling it off, aren't you?" he demanded. "You think it's too soon?"

When I said nothing, Eddie continued. "It's been ten fucking years."

"I know how long it's been," I replied angrily. "You just don't understand."

"I understand perfectly!" Eddie shouted back, shaking his

head. "You had a wife. She died. Ever since, you've been fucking miserable. Now you've gotten together with a woman you've known since you were a kid—a woman you were crazy about— and you want to pull the plug. Un-fucking-believable."

I did not respond. I looked down at the bar. I knew Eddie was right. Being with Becky was the first time I had been really happy since Melissa's death. Marriage was supposed to be until death do us part. Melissa and I had parted when she died. It was therefore not cheating or being unfaithful. Yet, I still felt guilty.

A part of me wanted to explore a relationship with Becky. Another part of me just could not bear to fully let Melissa go. I knew I had to do one or the other, but the choice was just not that easy.

I must have been completely lost in thought. When Eddie spoke again, I noticed he had come around the bar and was sitting on the barstool next to me. There was a glass in front of me with two inches of what I assumed was Glendalough. Eddie put his arm around my neck and shoulders and leaned in.

"Connor, I loved Mitzy too and I miss her," he said, "but she's gone. You deserve to be happy, and if Mitzy were here, she'd agree with me."

"If she were here, she'd tell you to stop fucking calling her Mitzy."

"Yeah, she would," Eddie laughed, "but she would agree with me, and you know it. Give whatever you have with Becky a chance. If it fails, so be it. But if it works, you can have a fucking life."

I didn't say a word. I just reached over, picked up the glass of whiskey, and held it up toward Eddie in a toast. As I brought the glass to my mouth to take a sip, my phone rang. I put the drink down and pulled out my cell. It was Becky calling. I slid my finger across the screen and answered.

"Hey, you on the way?" I asked.

The voice that answered was not Becky's. It was a man's voice that resonated with unbridled hatred and sent icy shivers of fear down my entire body. "Your girlfriend's not coming, Phelan."

24

I knew immediately that I was talking to Charles Edward Duncan, but the full impact of his words took a few seconds to sink in. As it did, my mind began to race. *He had Becky. Was she alive? Was she dead? If that son of a bitch hurt her...*

"Did you hear me, Phelan?" Duncan growled again, snapping me back to full attention.

"I heard you, Duncan. What have you done with her?" I demanded.

"She's perfectly safe... for now," he said slowly and ominously, enunciating every syllable, "but she won't be unless you do exactly as I say."

"Let her go, Duncan," I replied. "I'll do whatever you ask."

"You think I'm stupid?" he shouted back. "What I did to your pretty little secretary was nothing compared to what I'll do to Blondie here. I thought you would have understood my message."

I realized in that moment that I had been a fool. I assumed that Casey's attack was the result of me not being there. Now I understood that she had been the actual target. It was part of his overall plan to get to me. I should have seen it. It was right in front of my face, and I missed it. Instead of coming for me directly, Duncan was targeting the women closest to me. Now Becky might pay the ultimate price for my stupidity. I would have to play this killer's sick game and play it completely by his rules. He was pulling all the strings and I was his fucking puppet.

I took a deep breath and tried to calm myself before speaking again. "What do you want me to do?" I asked.

"That's better," he answered immediately. "You will come alone and unarmed. No cops. No surveillance. No weapons. You got it?"

"I understand," I said as I tried to maintain my composure. "Just tell me when and where."

"Go to where it all began," Duncan said, his voice dropping to an intimidating whisper. "You have one hour."

I had no idea what he meant, but before I could say another word, the line went dead. My frustration boiled over. "Son of a bitch!" I yelled as I pounded my fist down on the bar.

Eddie was still standing next to me. I quickly told him about the conversation.

"Can I do anything?" he asked.

"No," I said, "I have to go alone or he'll kill Becky."

"You don't think this fruit loop will keep his word, do you?" Eddie asked, "He'll kill her right after he fucking kills you."

"I know that, but what choice do I have?"

"Let me call the cops." He started to walk toward the old-fashioned pay phone in the corner of the bar.

I grabbed him by his arm and pulled him back toward me. "No," I warned, looking him straight in the eye. "No cops. I have to do this myself."

Eddie stared at me for a few seconds before he spoke again. "Fine. Just be careful, Clubber. I know you're this kung fu black belt—"

"Judo," I corrected.

"Whatever!" he shouted. "You're not fucking invincible and this guy is fucking nuts."

I appreciated what he was saying. Eddie was great for cursing and his advice was usually on the money. Expressing his own feelings, however, was not his forte. Telling me to be careful was about as tender as he got.

I extended my hand. He took it and as we shook, I put my free hand on his shoulder. "I'll be okay, boss," I said, trying to assure him. "Just don't call the cops."

Eddie was clearly not comfortable with my request. He looked away, so I squeezed his hand a little harder until he looked back at me.

"Promise me," I insisted.

"Fine," he said in a resigned voice as he let go of my hand. "I won't call the cops."

I headed for the door. I stopped in the doorway and looked back. Eddie was still standing in front of the bar, a look of concern on his face.

"Thanks, Eddie," I said, "I'll be okay."

"Hey, it's your fucking head," he replied as I walked out of the door.

I got in my Cherokee and started driving. The problem was that I had absolutely no idea where to go. *Go to where it all began,* he had said. What did that mean? Did he mean where the killings began?

I thought about it and decided that I would start at my office. I picked my office for two reasons. First, I thought that since he attacked Casey there, maybe that was where his assault on me had begun.

Second, if I was wrong, all my files on the Rockfield Strangler were there. Perhaps the key to his cryptic clue was there.

I stepped on the gas and sped toward my office. I made it there in less than ten minutes. I parked on the street and quickly walked to the front entrance. The door was marked with police tape and it was very obvious that no one had gone through since the tape had been applied.

I went around back. The parking lot was deserted and the back door had similar undisturbed police tape. I looked up the steps at the door to the upstairs apartment. It was closed, but there was no sign of any police tape.

I climbed the steps. The door was locked. I used my key and entered. The apartment was as silent as a tomb. Nothing seemed out of place, so I went down into the office. There were remnants of fingerprint powder on some of the walls and on Casey's desk. I cautiously checked the entire office. It was deserted. I had chosen incorrectly.

I took my files from my desk and starting scanning them, hoping to find something to solve the riddle. *Go to where it all began*, I thought. But where did it all begin? Where had what began? He obviously didn't mean the effort to kill me. That was here and I was clearly the only one here.

As I kept combing through page after page, my frustration overwhelmed me. I took out my phone again. I called Becky's number. Maybe I could get him back on the phone and get more information. The phone rang four times and Becky's cheery recorded voice told me that she couldn't answer my call, but she would call me back as soon as possible.

I disconnected the call and hoped Becky would be able to call me again, though as soon as possible seemed like a long way away.

I went back to my files, but after a few minutes, I found that I was rereading the same information over and over again. I slammed the file folder shut. The clock was ticking and I needed to figure out my next step or just take a guess.

Go to where it all began. The words echoed through my head. He hadn't meant killing me, but maybe he meant where he started all the killings. I threw open the file again and pulled out the police report on the murder of Kim Garrett. She was his first victim. I jotted down the address of the diner where she worked and where her body had been found in the parking lot.

I decided to take the files with me in case this was another wrong guess. I ran out the back door and went through the police tape. I swore as I pulled the tape off me, but didn't stop. I tossed the files onto the passenger seat and climbed back into my Cherokee. The tires squealed as I accelerated out of the parking lot. As I drove, I looked at the clock on my dashboard. I had forty minutes left on my deadline. I stepped down harder on the gas.

Within ten minutes, I pulled into the lot of the diner where Garrett had been murdered. I knew almost immediately that this was not the right place. The diner was open and the lot mostly full. It was not exactly the place for a killer to arrange a rendezvous.

I pulled into an open spot. Coming here had been foolish. I thought, *I've been doing some very stupid things lately.* If Becky was going to survive, I had to get my head out of my ass.

I closed my eyes and tried to concentrate. I tried to put myself into Duncan's shoes. Maybe then I could figure out what he meant. In truth, I didn't think it would be that hard for me to do. I remembered how much it had bothered me when I recognized the similarities between us. I had been close to the road Duncan had taken. The key to both of our downfalls was the death of our wives and children. Neither of us could face our loss. I had shut my life down, whereas Duncan had started taking lives.

My eyes opened as I realized that I had the answer. It all began for Duncan when his wife died. I reached over and grabbed one of the files. It seemed to take forever until I finally found the accident report. The site of the car accident was just outside the city of Hudson on the other side of the river. I would have enough time to get there, but if I was wrong, the odds were that Becky would die.

I drove as fast as felt I could get away with. If I went too fast, I would get pulled over and I just didn't have the time for that. I drove over the Rip Van Winkle Bridge and turned toward Hudson. As I drove, I tried to come up with a strategy for dealing with Duncan, but could not. It was painfully obvious to me that there was no way to plan anything. This was his game and I was a pathetic pawn. I would have to make things up on the fly. I hoped it would be enough.

It was almost forty-five minutes into my deadline when I arrived at the location of the fatal accident. It was a largely deserted area. It was a perfect place to plan an ambush. I looked around, but saw absolutely no one.

Tired of playing games, I shouted out, "Duncan! I'm here," and waited. There was no answer, so I yelled again. Still nothing.

The silence was abruptly broken by a shrill beeping sound that caused me to nearly jump out of my socks. I quickly realized that the sound was my cell phone ringing. A quick check of the screen confirmed the caller. I answered.

"I'm here, Duncan," I said menacingly. "Where the hell are you?"

"You're not here, Phelan," Duncan's voice hissed. "If you were, I would see you."

"I'm where it all started, pal," I replied. "I'm where your wife died."

"That's not where it started!" he screamed, his soft voice changing to raging anger. "That's where it all ended."

"What?" I said, unable to think of anything else.

Before I could say another word, Duncan screamed, "She dies in fifteen minutes," and hung up the phone.

What had he meant? I had been certain that everything had started for him when and where his wife died. But he had said that this was where everything ended. If where his wife died was where it all ended, then where was where it all started?

The answer came to me quickly. He had not been talking about the murders at all. He was talking about his life with his wife. I had been focusing on his killing spree, but he had been talking about the life he had lost.

I ran back to my Cherokee and grabbed my files. I tore through the pages, hoping to find the answer. As I looked, I could almost hear a clock ticking in my head as Becky's time slipped away. After about a minute or two, I found something. One of the reports that mentioned Duncan's wife identified her as an employee of Reliance Bank in Hudson.

I recalled that Duncan had been the head teller at the same bank. That must have been where they met. It was an assumption, but it was all I had. I took note of the address, hopped back in the driver's seat, and drove away.

I knew where the old Reliance Bank building was. I could get there in time, so long as I avoided any traffic problems. The bank closed years ago and had been abandoned ever since. It was a place Duncan knew well. He would have every advantage over me.

I arrived at the bank with less than five minutes to spare. As I approached it, I could see into the parking lot. Duncan's Plymouth Scamp was parked there. I was in the right place. That was the good news. The bad news was that I was probably going to die here.

I pulled into the lot and parked my Cherokee right in front of the Scamp. I might not survive, but Duncan was not going to be able to drive away. It was not much consolation. One way or the other, this matter was ending here.

I got out and walked to the main entrance directly in front of me. All the windows were covered with plywood, as were the glass panes in the door. When I got close enough, I could see that the door was slightly ajar. I pushed it and it opened slightly with a creak. I waited for a few seconds, but nothing happened.

The inside of the building was pitch-black. However, I could see a faint flickering glow some distance ahead of me. I walked in and closed the door behind me. When I did, I heard the lock click.

All around me was dark now. The way in was locked. I had nowhere to go but toward the strange glow. I took a deep breath and started forward.

25

I walked toward the eerie glow. As my eyes adjusted to the darkness, I could make out that I was in a narrow hallway that went toward the far wall before turning sharply left. Whatever was giving off the light was somewhere beyond that turn.

When I was close enough, I carefully looked around the corner. I saw the source of the light and my breath caught in my throat. Beyond was the main part of the old bank. It was a wide-open room with high ceilings. There were three tables on the left side that had once been used by patrons to write out their checks and deposit slips. To the right, a long wooden counter ran almost the length of the room. There were four or five spaces where tellers once sat. These windows had wrought iron bars allowing only a small opening.

On all the tables to the left and running along the entire counter on the right were lighted kerosene lamps, just like the ones in Duncan's home. Their flickering flames illuminated most of the room and reflected almost hauntingly off the marble walls.

"It's about time, Phelan," an angry voice called out, startling me.

I looked in the direction of the voice and saw Duncan. At the far end of the room was a stone staircase that rose to a landing. Each stair had lighted candles on the far left and right. Duncan stood at the edge of the landing dressed entirely in black, his face appearing demonic from the glow of the candles and lanterns. Behind him was the old bank vault.

I walked toward him and stopped at the base of the stairs.

"I'm here, Duncan," I called out. "Where is she?"

He said nothing for a few seconds before breaking into a malevolent grin. He turned and grabbed the handle of the vault door and pulled. It swung open revealing Becky. She was tied to an old wooden chair at the ankles and across the chest. She was gagged and terror was etched on her face.

The moment I saw her, I felt a surge of white-hot anger. "You son of a bitch," I growled and started up the stairs.

Duncan immediately pulled out a hunting knife, its blade twinkling in the light, and put it to Becky's throat. I stopped my ascent.

"Get back down to the bottom of the stairs or she dies!" Duncan screamed.

I put up my hands in surrender and backed down the stairs. When I reached the bottom, Duncan put the knife in his back pocket, stepped forward away from Becky, and spoke again.

"We are doing this my way, Talisman," he said, his shark-like eyes focused on me, yet also not quite there either.

"Why do you call me Talisman?" I asked, hoping that if I could keep him talking, I might figure a way out of this predicament.

"Don't play coy with me!" he roared back. "You are the second Talisman of evil. Allen was the first, but you are the last. And when you are finished, I will be free of it forever."

Free of what? I wondered. But before I could solve the riddle, Duncan pulled something out of his other back pocket and tossed it to me. I reached up and caught it. It was a pair of metal handcuffs.

"Put those on," he ordered, "or she dies."

I knew that if my hands were cuffed, my chances of survival were slim. I had to find a way to stall him. Unfortunately, Duncan was obviously thinking the same thing because when I hesitated, he again pulled out the knife and started toward Becky.

"No need to threaten her again!" I shouted. He stopped and looked at me suspiciously. I clicked the first handcuff on my left wrist.

"Now the other," he grunted.

I grabbed the other cuff and was about to put it on my other wrist when he called out again.

"No, no," he said, "behind your back."

I stared hard at him. "How do I know you'll let her go if I do?" I asked.

"You don't," he replied instantly, "but I guarantee you that I will cut her throat if you don't."

I had no choice. I put my hands behind me and started putting the right cuff on. I made sure only to slide the arm of the restraint far enough for the ratchet to click just once. This meant that I was handcuffed, but might have a chance to pull out one of my hands. It was a lousy plan, but I had nothing else. I just hoped Duncan didn't check them too closely.

"Turn around," he barked. "Show me that they're really on."

I turned around, but made sure that he could see more of my left side. I shook my hands back and forth to show they were bound. Then I turned to face him.

Duncan said nothing for several seconds, though it seemed longer. "Now," he said in a demanding though confident voice, "on your knees."

I did as he asked, though I made sure to curl my toes so I

could leap to my feet if need be. Duncan flashed that wicked smile and started walking down the stairs. The entire building was silent except for the faint sound of his shoes on the stairs. He eventually reached the bottom of the stairs and stood in front of me, looking down in triumph.

"At last," he said, his voice sliding out with his breath, "ultimate release."

He inhaled deeply and closed his eyes. As the seconds passed, Duncan started to tremble. His face showed signs of fear and terror, and he began mumbling to himself. "Oh, Sarah... no..." Tears flowed down his cheeks and his trembling intensified.

At once, I understood. Duncan was reliving the death of his wife. He was bringing all his emotion, his pain, and his anguish to the surface. He was bringing it all out of himself in anticipation of killing me. He was going to sacrifice me like a lamb slaughtered on an altar. In his distorted mind, he thought that my death—the death of the evil talisman—would end his suffering. Maybe it was the scary similarity between our lives and the terrible loss we each suffered. Whatever the reason, I just knew.

Suddenly, he threw his head back and screamed. It was a bloodcurdling yell that sent icy-cold shivers down my spine. The scream was still echoing through the ceiling when I lunged at him. My hands were restrained behind me, so I led with my head and right shoulder. My shoulder slammed into his solar plexus and he fell backward.

I went to the floor with him, but could not control my landing. My head hit one of the stone steps and I saw stars. I tried to stand, but the nausea and dizziness from my concussion made it very difficult. The stitches above my eye must have come apart because I felt a lot of blood flowing down my face.

When I was finally able to stand, Duncan was waiting for

me. If it was possible, the look in his eyes was even more sinister. His face was so contorted with rage that he was barely recognizable. He charged at me with his hands outstretched.

I stepped to my right and put the bottom of my left foot on his ankle as he advanced, causing him to stumble and fall. He landed flat on his stomach.

As Duncan struggled to rise, I began pulling on my right hand, trying to get it out of the cuff. It should have come loose, but didn't. My hand came partially out, but the fleshy part of my thumb was stuck in the arm of the restraint. I pulled as hard as I could. I felt the metal of the cuff dig into my flesh and my hand became wet with blood.

In my effort to free my hands, I failed to notice that Duncan was on his feet. He grabbed me by the shoulder, spun me around slightly, and punched me square in the jaw. I spun with the momentum of the punch and fell to the floor. The left side of my face smacked the stone and it nearly knocked me out.

He grabbed me by the hair and yanked me up. I tried to resist, but my strength was failing. I had gotten to my knees when I felt Duncan's arm come across my throat. I instinctively turned my head toward his elbow to avoid what I knew was coming. I was not quick enough and Duncan began choking me.

His technique was poor, but he was surprisingly strong. He also had his weight on me and his head leaned in by my ear. It gave me very little room to maneuver. Without my hands, I wasn't sure I could escape from the choke.

As the seconds went by, I could feel myself fading. If I did not break loose in the next thirty or forty seconds, I would lose consciousness and die.

"Let me hear your last breath," Duncan whispered in my ear. "Die, Talisman."

Panic began to set in. For the first time, I thought that I was not going to make it. Darkness was creeping in from my peripheral vision and I would soon black out.

They say that your life passes before your eyes when you are near death. That didn't happen for me. Instead, the only thing on my mind at that moment was that if I died, this maniac would kill Becky too.

I could hear my earlier question and his answer echoing in my mind.

How do I know you'll let her go if I do?

You don't.

Becky and I would never get the chance to explore this new relationship. I hadn't been happy in a very long time, but maybe now I could be. For the first time in years, I was thinking not about a past that I could never change, but of living for the present and the future, both of which seemed very appealing. I had to find a way to survive. I was not going to die like this.

I felt a rush of adrenaline as I dug deep into my last remaining strength. Duncan apparently sensed this. He grunted as he tried to squeeze even harder and leaned more of his weight on me. When I felt him put all his weight on me, I knew I had one final chance to live. I made a sudden movement forward and down. This caused Duncan to be off balance for just a second. He felt it and reacted by leaning back and pulling me upward. This was exactly what I wanted him to do.

I went with his movement and was able to get the balls of my feet under me. I pushed up as hard as I could. As I did, my right hand finally broke free. Duncan fell backward and I landed on top of him.

I rolled off him and forced myself to stand. Duncan got to his feet at almost the same time. He came right at me and threw a wild right cross. I could use my hands now, and was ready for him. I blocked his punch and struck him in the face with the heel of my right hand. His head snapped back, but he did not go down. He lunged at me again with both of his hands reaching for my neck.

I grabbed him by his wrists and pulled his arms straight up. I raised my foot to his stomach and fell backward. As I rolled, I extended my leg and Duncan flipped over me and landed on his back with a thump. I could hear the air come out of his lungs when he hit the ground. I thought the fight was over, but it took only a second or two for him to start moving again. It was a race to see who could stand first.

I was just a hair quicker, so I was prepared when Duncan attacked again. He tried to kick me in the groin. I stepped back on my right foot and turned my body. This allowed me to catch his foot with both of my hands. I twisted his ankle as hard as I could. He screamed as the tendons and ligaments in his ankle snapped. I then stepped forward and flung him back as hard as I could.

He fell back two or three feet, and his head, neck, and upper back slammed hard into the counter, causing the kerosene lamps on top to fall off. As they smashed, they each exploded in a fireball. One landed on the floor inches from Duncan. The explosion instantly ignited the front of Duncan's shirt. He howled and writhed in agony as it burned. He twisted and rolled on the floor, smothering the fire. Eventually, he lost consciousness and lay on his stomach, not moving.

I walked over to make sure Duncan was out and saw that the area behind the counter was carpeted. Two of the lamps had burst on it and fire was spreading rapidly across it. I turned and moved as quickly as I could toward the stairs and Becky. I didn't know whether or not the entire building was going to burn, but I had no intention of sticking around to find out.

When I got to the top of the stairs, Becky was still tied to the chair. She must have been struggling to free herself during the fight because one of her feet was loose from the ropes. I entered the vault, untied her, and pulled off her gag. She stood, turned back to me, put her arms around me, and held me tight. She was sobbing.

Though I wanted to hold her, I knew we had to get out of there quickly.

"Becky, we have to go," I said urgently, breaking our embrace. "The building is on fire."

She let me go and I pointed toward the stairs. We ran with Becky in front of me.

"Go down and stay to the right. The fire will be to your left," I said as we left the vault. "Once we get out of here, we can—"

I never finished my sentence. Becky screamed in terror.

Duncan was at the top of the stairs. He had either regained consciousness or had faked being unconscious. His face was severely burned with bright red splotches. His chest was blackened and charred. He was leaning on his left leg and dragging his broken right ankle behind him.

He had his hunting knife in his right hand over his head. He brought it down in a stabbing motion. I knew I couldn't block it. I grabbed Becky's right shoulder with both my hands and flung her away to the left. Though Becky was safe, I was wide open and vulnerable. I braced myself for the knife about to plunge into my chest.

The knife never hit me. Instead, a loud bang resounded through the building. Duncan visibly stiffened. He seemed to pause for a second before falling. He tumbled all the way to the bottom and landed at the feet of Dom Bryce, who stood with his Colt 45 at the ready.

Dom knelt down and put his fingers on Duncan's neck to check for a pulse. He looked up at me and ran his fingers across his throat to signal that Charles Edward Duncan was dead.

26

Things happened quickly after Dom helped Becky and me out of the burning building. He walked us both over to his truck, lowered the tailgate, and instructed us to sit. He then took out his cell phone and made a series of calls.

Within minutes, there were multiple fire trucks, police cars, and ambulances at the scene. Though it had appeared to me that the old bank was going to burn to the ground, the fire department had the fire contained and put it out quickly. Becky and I watched them set up their hoses and enter the building while paramedics worked on us.

Becky had a bruise on her neck. She explained that Duncan had grabbed her from behind and choked her right in the parking lot of The Cardinal. She went unconscious and awoke in the back of his car with her hands tied behind her. He had dragged her into the bank and tied her up exactly as I found her. She had some rope burns on her wrists as well. Fortunately, that was the extent of the physical damage.

I was not so lucky. In addition to aggravating my concussion, almost every stitch above my eye had come loose. The front of my shirt and most of my face was stained with blood. I also had a laceration on my hand from where the handcuff ripped my skin apart. I was given large bandages on my hand and eye. The one on my eye completely covered it.

The paramedic was almost done with me when I saw Dom, multiple police officers, and the county coroner come out of the bank carrying a long, black body bag. They placed it into a waiting hearse.

I found it odd that as much as I despised Charles Edward Duncan, I also slightly sympathized with him. I understood the terrible loss he suffered and the agony of realizing that the rest of his life would be without the wife and child he had planned to spend it with.

Like him, I had shut down my life completely and retreated from everything I knew. I quit my job, threw myself into a position in New York City that I absolutely hated, and spent most of my time alone in a Manhattan studio apartment. I simply ran away from my pain, hoping it would never find me.

Charles Edward Duncan had channeled his anger and rage into a murderous rampage. His rage at the world boiled inside him and he released it by killing women. His pain and internal suffering overwhelmed him and stripped him of his sanity.

I pondered at just how similar we both were. The aftermath of our personal tragedies and loss forever scarred and changed us. Neither of us had handled the aftermath well, and I wondered how close I might have been to losing my sanity and perhaps walking on the path Duncan had chosen.

Just then, almost as if reading my mind, Becky slid next to me and embraced me. She looked into my uncovered eye and smiled. Despite everything going on around me and the nearly unbearable headache I was experiencing, I smiled back. I had one thing Duncan would never have—a second chance at love and life. I didn't know whether Becky and I were headed for heartbreak or happily ever after. What I did know was that I wanted to take the journey with her and find out. We said nothing. Words were not necessary.

A little over an hour later, I found myself once again lying in a hospital bed at the Rockfield Medical Center. When I arrived in the emergency room, my doctor put new stitches over my eye. While he worked, he launched into an angry lecture when he heard about my recent activities while I was recovering from a concussion. He had made it clear that I was going to spend the next week in the hospital getting bed rest.

Becky and Casey were waiting for me when the nurses wheeled me into my room for the night. I had no idea how they had gotten my room number, but I was glad to see them. I relayed what the doctor had told me and was about to announce that I planned on going home in the morning, but the looks from Becky and Casey made it clear that I would be risking their wrath if I did so.

Becky explained to me that she had been treated and released. Casey was still spending the night for observation and said that her mother had mercifully gone home about ten minutes before I arrived.

"If I'm staying here, then so are you," Casey said accusingly, before smiling and saying, "Don't make me call my mother."

"Anything but that," I said, starting to laugh, which caused my head to nearly explode.

Becky came over and sat on the bed next to me. She smiled, but her eyes glistened with tears.

"Do I look that bad?" I joked.

"No," she answered immediately.

At almost the exact same time, Casey said, "Worse."

I shot Casey a dirty look and she shrugged innocently. I turned back to Becky.

She put her hands on either side of my face before speaking

again. "This is the second time you've been hurt because of me," she said, "and I don't want you to—"

"This was not because of you," I interrupted. "This was entirely because of me. Duncan went after both of you because he wanted to hurt me by attacking the people I cared about most."

"Well, you don't have to worry about him anymore," a loud voice boomed from the door. Dom Bryce was there with a huge smile on his face. "He's dead as a doorknob," Dom continued, "thanks to sweet Lorraine here." He reached down and patted the Colt 45 in his hip holster.

"Sweet Lorraine?" I asked sarcastically.

"Of course," Dom replied, "you always give your gun a woman's name."

"That's the only way he gets a woman on his hip," Casey interjected.

"Now just a minute," Dom shouted back.

My head rang like a gong when he shouted. Becky must have noticed because she instantly stepped between Dom and Casey. "Both of you cool it," she said in an angry whisper, her eyes inviting no debate. "Connor's got a bad headache and there will be no shouting. You got it?"

Casey said nothing, but raised her hands in surrender.

"Yes, ma'am," Dom replied with a smile.

A few minutes later, I decided to broach the one thing that had been bothering me ever since I saw Charles Duncan lying dead at Dom's feet.

"Dom, can I ask you something?"

"Anything," he answered.

"How did you know where to find me?" I asked. "And while I'm at it, how did you even know I was going after Duncan?"

Dom sat back in his chair and smiled. "Your buddy, Eddie,

called me and told me about that nut job kidnapping Becky and calling you on her phone."

I had to laugh to myself when I heard that. I couldn't be mad at Eddie for not following my instructions since I would be dead if he hadn't called Dom. Besides, I could almost hear Eddie's voice in my head saying, *I promised I wouldn't call the cops. I never said anything about calling Dom.*

I decided that I owed him a thank you and box seats to a Yankee game. Even though I hate the Yankees, I would even go to the game with him. I owed him no less.

"But Dom, how did you find me?" I asked, "I never told Eddie the clue Duncan gave me."

Dom looked momentarily puzzled. "I don't know what clue you're talking about," he said. "Eddie said the mutt called you using Becky's cell phone."

"Yeah, so?" I replied.

"I just contacted some of my fellow officers who haven't retired yet, and had them ping the phone," Dom said triumphantly. "It came back at the old bank building."

I thought about the one hour I spent driving all over creation trying to figure out Duncan's damn puzzle. "Wish I had thought of that," I said finally.

The four of us talked for quite a while. Eventually, I felt very tired and announced that I needed some sleep. We all said our goodbyes. I could hear Dom and Casey bickering back and forth as they walked out of the room and down the hall. The two of them just never seemed to stop.

Becky stayed behind. She came right up to me and hugged me tight. After a few seconds, she released me and gave me a long kiss. Then she flashed that incredible smile and said, "I'll see you tomorrow."

She walked out of the room and I found myself just looking

at the empty doorway. After a minute or two, I lay back and was asleep almost immediately.

When I awoke, I saw by the clock on the wall that it was almost three o'clock in the morning. I was about to go back to sleep when I heard a very soft sound. I rolled over to the other side of the bed. There was a large leather chair next to my bed. Becky was in the chair sleeping with a hospital blanket over her. She must have come back after I dozed off and decided to watch over me before falling asleep herself.

I stared at her for a long time. I knew in that moment that my life would never be the same.

CPSIA information can be obtained
at www.ICGtesting.com
Printed in the USA
JSHW051939060622
26742JS00010B/113